A GOSPEL GROTESQUE

A GOSPEL GROTESQUE

Photius Avant

For those of us who will die.

"Ever get the feeling you've been cheated?"

-Johnny Rotten

+++

First, it was warm.

Pulsating warmth radiated throughout his being, permeating all things with indescribable sweetness. A tenderness formed and guided the elements as they were woven together in him. Pre-consciousness lulled gently to consciousness. Emerging.

Then, it was bright.

Through closed eyelids it called to him. His silver eyes opened for the first time. A brilliant but gentle light illuminated all things. Shape. Color. Form. Movement. He looked down and saw his form. Awareness. Focus. There was will but not will alone. There was reason.

Then, there was the voice.

The dazzling light filled his eyes and his being with peace. The light was life. His life. From the light came the voice, pure and majestic.

"My beloved," said the voice. "You are Lucifer."

The newborn creature stood in pristine beauty, embraced by the resplendent light. "I am Lucifer," he responded gently.

"My beloved, you have been created for great things."

+++

The sound of thunder pooled out across the flat desert for miles. Gentle winds stirred the scrub bushes, sweeping sand over rock. Infernal heat gave way to a breeze promising relief. The blistered white earth yearned for anything the gray skies might be kind enough to give. All life reached upward, patiently waiting.

They hit the ground as one, sending up a massive cloud of sand and dust high into the air. The impact sent a shockwave tearing through the virgin desert, snapping branches and toppling rocks. Slowly, the wind diminished the cloud to a haze, revealing crumbled shapes on the ground. Ten. Thirty. Seventy. A hundred. Thousands. All white-robed, tattered, soiled, and singed. All stunned. Motionless. An army of dirty marble statues fallen down in the sand. One by one, they struggled to their feet, surveying their surroundings. Above all things, they were puzzled. No one spoke. Not even the Master. His silver eyes scanned and pierced the alien terrain, assessing the nature of the situation. Stooping, he plunged his hand into the sand and watched it pour out between his chalky fingers. Strange. The Elder watched him as he examined the sagebrush and fingered stones.

"Master," he started, hesitantly.

The Master paid no mind. He was transfixed on a black beetle climbing a cactus. How fascinating, and yet hideous to fathom. Gently, he lifted the beetle and cradled it in his hand. Such an intricate creature and so small. A protective shield, nimble legs, and formidable pincers at its mouth.

"Master, what is this place? Where...where are we?"

Incredible. And repulsive. Crawling on spindly legs. He pushed it onto its back and watched its mechanical legs scurry in a frenzy above its loathsome belly. Watching the helpless bug fight to regain its feet, a faint grin came to his lean face.

"My Lord, what…?"

He softly closed his fingers over the beetle, crushing it slowly. He opened his hand, studying the insect, its mangled body and fluids pressed against his white palm. A single antenna twitched and stopped. Dead. He fingered it a last time. Marvelous. Letting it fall to his feet, he wiped his hands on his dirty tunic and turned to the Elder.

"We stay here, Ba'al," he announced, studying the sky.

The Elder bowed, "Yes, Master. But where are we?" His mind was still racing.

"Far from where we started," he said dryly, turning a sharp glance at the Elder.

"Master, about the revolt…I am…"

"Forget it. Your strategy was a bit too bold, that's all." The Master placed a reassuring hand on the Elder's shoulder.

"If I may ask, Lord, what are your plans regarding another assault? Should we…"

"There will be plenty of time for that. You and the Others must be patient. This place is one of the Adversary's projects, and I am certain that it will prove useful to us."

Spotting a mountain on the horizon, the Master leaped to its top in a blink. Alone, he beheld vast expanses of mighty forests, undulating hills, and green plains. Reptiles of every size and shape ambled gracefully in herds, soared on massive membranous wings, skulked in pairs, or trudged alone. Desert or tropic, mountain or valley, sky or sea, every place on this curious sphere was saturated with life. But not unending life. Life based on need, governed by want. Life seeking to preserve and perpetuate itself. Life kindled by a spark but extinguishable in dust. The Elder appeared at his side.

"In the meantime, get comfortable, but watch carefully. As spectacular as this place is," he gazed into the distance, "I am sure it is still under construction."

+

"Shut up, bitch!" the tall centurion shouted as he struck her in the face. Hitting the ground, the woman's screams abated for only a second. Her husband, half a foot shorter than the soldier, tried to grab him by the throat but missed, scratching him instead. Shoving him away with his left hand, the soldier drew his sword with his right. "Is it your turn now, Jewish filth?" he spat.

That's right.

The ever present heat baked the chalky soil and sandy stone on the road to Sidon. An inconstant breeze occasionally nudged the branches of the cedars — more of a source of torment than relief. The natives accepted the weather as they accepted their own skin. It was the Romans who could never seem to adjust to summers in Palestine, which is why they

4

often compelled Jews to carry loads for them. A Jew said no only if he wanted to die.

"Titinius!" the stocky one broke in. "We're done here! I'll carry the gear! Let's move on!"

What did you do to stop him? Nothing...

The tall soldier stared down his blade into the eyes of the pathetic bearded scum before him. Neither one blinked, their eyes ablaze with hatred. Despite his fury, tears welled in the Jew's eyes.

"The Lord of hosts, the one true God, will call you to account for this," he uttered through clenched teeth, pointing an accusing leathery finger at his armored enemy.

"Another word from you, and I'll have your tongue and your eyes," the centurion said, baring his yellow teeth and pressing the tip of his sword into the Jew's cheek, drawing blood.

He is not Roman. He is not human.

The woman erupted into screaming sobs again. Crawling through the dirt and rocks, she reached the little body. She howled as only a mother can. A girl of eight lay still on her back, her face pale except for the blood spattered on her chin. Glassy eyes the color of almonds stared sightlessly above. Above her stood a muscular centurion cleaning his sword on his cloak. His eyes were empty, and yet his face revealed a sense of relief.

That felt good, didn't it?

The wailing woman gathered her child in her arms, rocking back and forth, their raven black hair blowing as banners of misery and defeat on the bitter breeze. She screamed, bringing the gentle face to hers. The empty-eyed soldier inspected his blade carefully. Spotless. An itch pricked the back of his neck.

How about another one? It has been over a month.

"Julian!" the stocky one pleaded. "Let's go!"

You stood there and watched him. You did nothing.

"Come on, Julian," said the tall soldier, taking neither eye nor sword away from the Jew. "Let's move on."

The centurion with the empty eyes turned to the wailing mother. Streaming tears mingled with blood and sweat, catching wisps of black hair. The stocky one picked up the soldiers' load, shifting its weight onto his back. "Titinius?" Breaking his stare at the Jew, the tall soldier lowered his sword, taking a step back toward the empty-eyed soldier. The Jew did not move. As the woman cried, cradling her lifeless child, the itch moved from the back of the empty-eyed soldier's neck to a place inside him, which could not be scratched.

Just a little more.

With his right hand, he grabbed the woman's hair, prying her face away from the child's. He raised his sword.

That's it.

The Jew screamed unintelligibly, lunging for the centurion with fresh blood on his sword and hands. Stepping quickly into his path, the tall soldier buried his sword to the hilt in the Jew's chest. Their eyes met again in pure animosity.

"He will call you to account," the Jew whispered.

He fell, leaving the tall soldier holding a sword smeared with blood.

The empty-eyed soldier cleaned his sword on his cloak once again, returning it to its sheath, and then he wiped his hands. Going down on one knee, the tall one cleaned his sword on the Jew's tunic. He stood, putting it away.

"Commodian, set down the load for a minute, and move this one, will you," ordered the tall one, pointing to the father.

"Move him where?"

"To the side of the road, you ignorant bastard. We can't leave three corpses in the middle of the road."

"You killed him. You move him," the stocky one replied coldly.

You just stood there.

The tall soldier stepped rapidly, indignantly, towering over the stocky one, their faces not six inches apart. "I am your superior officer, and I am giving you an order. Move the body, or I will have you flogged, damn you." The stench of his breath tasted of stomach rot and onions.

Loosening his grip on the load, the stocky soldier let it fall to the ground with a clunk. He bent over the dead Jew, using his fingers to close the corpse's accusing black eyes. They never fully closed. Taking him by the ankles, he dragged the Jew's body over the uneven rocks, his limp arms

7

forming a frame for the pool of blood over his head. With each heavy step backward, the trail of blood diminished, though the stocky soldier tried not to look. The tall centurion dragged the woman to the ditch in a few quick strides as if he was moving a load of rubbish to a dung heap.

Just a Jew.

Effortlessly, the empty-eyed centurion pulled the little girl's body by a single wrist like a doll, face down over the rocks. At the bottom of the ditch, he removed his sword again.

A reminder.

"By Jupiter, Mars, and Apollo, what are you doing, Julian?!" shouted the stocky one.

Don't get on your high horse, now. What did you do when Julian grabbed that girl? Why didn't you defend her?

A lock of hair from the girl. A lock of hair from the mother. The empty-eyed soldier put them in a pouch on his belt.

Put them with the others at home.

The slaughtered family lay scattered in full view at the bottom of the ditch. Soaked in blood. Bathed in dust. Baking and soon to bloat in the Palestinian summer sun. The three soldiers took a last look at the bodies. Horror. Pride. Satisfaction. Silence. Dust in the eyes from the cruel breeze.

On the road above them stood the three unseen Voices smiling with cold eyes, admiring their work.

"Give a full report to the Master, Moloch."

"To the Master himself? Why not the Elder?"

"The Master has the Elder at work on something else right now. He doesn't want him disturbed. He personally asked me to have all reports sent to him until further notice."

"As you wish, Chemosh." The reporter vanished, leaving the two Voices quietly watching the soldiers walk down the road toward the city. Unaffected by the heat, the Voices stood in leisurely silence for several moments. Finally, the soldiers disappeared from view.

"Do you think we will be doing this forever, Ahiram?"

"It's difficult to say. We have seen creatures of all different kinds completely wiped out before. The giant reptiles come to mind. I don't see how humans are any different."

"Personally, I think it will take a while before we eliminate them all. They are resilient"

"But predictable."

A knowing silence. Flies began to gather around the bodies, landing on arms and faces that gave no protest. The Voices followed the flies' movements with their golden eyes.

"At times, it is too easy."

"At times," he conceded, reflecting. "But always rewarding."

They vanished, leaving the destroyed family to the heat and the flies.

+

Since the Master was seldom in one place for very long, the reporter inquired of three Voices and two Tormentors as to his location. Once again, he was outside the Temple at Jerusalem. The naked midday sun bore down heavily upon the cramped crowds pressing toward and away from the Temple. Sacrificial smoke and sweat thickened the air. Like a lizard, the reporter scaled the wall of an adjacent building for a better view. There he was. By the money changers and animal vendors. Leaping to his side, the reporter bowed.

"My Lord, news from myself, Chemosh, and Ahiram." He kept his head bowed until the Master spoke.

Not turning to face him, the Master spoke flatly. "Proceed."

"Our assignments Julian, Titinius, and Commodian have made unexpected progress. Julian murdered a little girl and her mother in cold blood. Titinius killed the father, who was unarmed. And Commodian passively watched it all."

"Good," said the Master, beginning to walk slowly past the money changers toward the animal vendors. The reporter followed. Inspecting the animals, the Master began, "Titinius is a nationalist. Build on that. What he did, he did for Rome. Do not stop at getting him to justify his actions; make sure he feels proud of them. More opportunities like this will certainly present themselves." He stooped to scratch several of the lambs sharply with his finger. Just a little blemish before the sacrifice.

"Very good, my Lord."

"Commodian's conscience is undoubtedly bothering him," the Master continued. "Give him a few days of wine and prostitutes. When the pain comes back, give him more. Crush him with guilt. Do not let him get up. He will dissipate. Hopefully, you can get a suicide from him." He stood, moving toward the turtledoves in their wooden cages.

"And Julian, Master?"

"Julian is well on his way. A fine specimen among these vermin, actually. He is hollow. We have taken his conscience and his regard for human life. He is so numb that killing is the only thing he really enjoys now. Give him the itch as often as you can."

"Certainly, Lord."

"Keep me abreast of any developments or complications, Moloch. That is all."

"Yes, my Lord." He bowed and was gone.

The Master had not walked three steps before another reporter appeared before him, bowing.

"Let's hear it."

"News regarding Herod Antipas, my…"

"I know what you're working on," he snapped. "Let's hear it!"

"The Baptist hasn't got long before Antipas puts him in prison, my Lord."

Turning fully to face the reporter, the Master said, "A paltry win at best. Little Herod isn't quite as savage as his father, otherwise John would already be dead. Even in prison, it is doubtful that Antipas would lay a finger on the mangy bastard."

"Then, how should we proceed, Master?"

"Use Antipas' lust to your advantage."

"How so, my Lord?"

The Master walked slowly back to the money changers, the reporter following.

He began, "He stole his brother's wife and took her *and* her twelve-year-old daughter into his house. From what you've told me before, he has his eye on the girl, too. The new wife hates John and wants him dead, but that is not enough."

"My Lord, I fail to see…"

"Use the daughter, you imbecile!" he hissed. "Build on his desire for her, slowly, but do not allow him to touch her. He can satisfy his urges on Herodias. Now," he paused, "she knows about his affinity for the girl?"

"Yes, Master."

"Use that. Build tension within him for the girl. She will be the key to the Baptist's death. Little Herod's birthday is in six months. Before he passes out from drunkenness, prompt Herodias to get the girl to ask him for John's head. Have her do a little dance for him first, just to get his blood pumping."

The reporter bowed. "I understand, Lord."

"You *understand*, of course, that the more these apes are addicted to their passions, the easier they are to control."

"Of course, my Lord."

"The Baptist poses no threat to us. It's just that his talk about repentance makes it a little less fun for all of us."

"Certainly, Master," he bowed.

"That is all."

So many affairs to manage. Fortunately, the Master had as much time as he needed. He never rested. He never grew weary. Tirelessly, he set pieces in motion, watched them collide, rejoiced as they fell, and exulted when they were smashed to bits. Yet again, it was time to watch the pieces move. The Master leaped.

China. Luoyang, the Royal City. With the restoration of the Han family to the imperial throne came the obligatory execution of those who supported the throne's usurper. Or worked for him. The unhappy men waited in chains in a single file line. Rain pelted them, loosening months of dirt, soaking their filthy clothes. There was only one executioner, so his sword would have a busy day.

Gaul. A nameless hillside. Seventy-one young warriors lay dead or near death in brittle brown grass. An ambitious warrior had sought to assert himself over the current, stale authority. Men picked sides and bled in battle. The new order was in place, until a hidden rival poisoned the new chieftain's drink. More blood absorbed by the dirt.

Hejaz. A drying wadi. Two companies of slave traders hacked and stabbed into one another after one company leader accused the other of breaking their agreement. The bigger group prevailed and inspected the now unowned cargo — twenty-one young women aged fourteen through twenty-one and five boys aged seven through thirteen. The leader instructed the others to tie the women with their group of forty. With raised voices and cracking whips, they followed orders. He commanded them to leave the boys to him.

Kingdom of the Maya. The pinnacle of the pyramid temple of Palenque. Four muscular young men held a terrified war prisoner on his back, stretched across the altar. The turquoise bejeweled priest muttered incantations and raised his obsidian knife. A string of sudden fevers had struck down over three hundred people, young and old, strong and weak. The gods were almost certainly angry about something and needed to be appeased. Down plunged the knife.

Samaria. A poor farmer's house. A young man sat crestfallen by his wife as she slept, placing his hand on hers. Once an ethereal beauty and the envy of every woman in the surrounding villages, the sickness had wasted the young woman nearly to her bones. Her breath was shallow. An elderly man with a peppered beard, the young farmer's father, came to his side, placing a gentle hand on his head, urging him to pray. Slapping the hand away, the young man raged that he had prayed. And prayed. And prayed some more. If God was listening, then surely he did not care that such a good young woman wasted away in agony. Where was God? Nowhere.

Moving. Falling. Smashing. The pieces swayed according to the Master's plans. There were often complications, of course. After all, the Adversary had agents at work for him, but it seemed that the Master always got the upper hand. Stepping outside the house in Samaria, the Master looked into the sun, the silver of his eyes shining brilliantly. His eyes did not hurt as human eyes. He beheld flares and spots dancing upon the majestic star. Nothing escaped his notice.

Reaching into his tunic, he produced a tiny leather bag. He opened it and emptied its contents into his hand. Apple seeds. Slowly, he caressed the seeds, still fresh, moving them about in his palm. The memory arose within him with crystalline clarity:

An aged couple stumbled through the wilderness, holding onto one another. The matted off-white masses of hair pouring down their backs and shoulders framed their haggard dark faces. Covered in layers of old animal skins, they seemed burdened. Their halting movements revealed fatigue. Their sunken eyes revealed sorrow too wide and too deep to comprehend.

The Master closed his hand, clutching the seeds tightly. He returned them to the bag, which he again buried in his tunic. Compelled to see his collection of trophies again, he leaped to the Keep.

+

Darkness ruled the Keep. Immovable and suffocating darkness. What would have been the sky was an abyss, which no light had ever pierced. It pressed down upon the innumerable prisoners scattered and crowded beneath it. They had never seen one another, although some had stood beside one another for eons. New prisoners arrived every moment, stumbling through the blackness. The older prisoners remained motionless, having learned the futility of movement long ago. Although most of them stared ahead with sightless eyes, some looked upward, still seeing nothing, but hoping for some kind of deliverance.

The Guardian stood watching atop the east wall of the Keep. He never blinked once in all the ages since he was given charge of the first prisoners, and he had never lost even one. It was impossible. Only he, the Master, and Others like them could see down here. The Keep was a flat, featureless expanse stretching out endlessly in all directions. Seamless walls ten stories tall ran from horizon to horizon in each direction. Any prisoner groping along a seemingly interminable wall would eventually, after ages of desperate search, only find another wall and have what little hope was left crushed beneath the weight of eternity.

Soundlessly, the Master arrived behind the Guardian. Sensing his presence, the Guardian turned and bowed. "My Lord." The Master looked out over the prisoners. Of all places, the Keep was his favorite. Seeing what was left of human beings in their rightful place, suspended in darkness as insects in amber, sent a warm satisfaction through him. This was true happiness.

"Where are the newest arrivals, Ashteroth?" he asked, searching the faces of prisoners in motion.

"Just beneath us at the wall here, Master." The Guardian pointed to a space at the base of the wall just to the right. There, the Master saw the Judean family murdered only hours before. Father, mother, and child embraced one another, their faces turned to the abyss above.

The father prayed, "*Blessed art Thou, O Lord God of our fathers, and blessed and glorified be Thy name forever. Amen. Let Thy mercy be upon us, O Lord, as we have set our hope in Thee.*"

The Master smiled.

The father's prayer continued.

"*Blessed art Thou, O Lord, teach me Thy statutes...*"

Amusing.

"Such a strange thing," the Guardian pondered.

"What exactly?"

"The manner in which the Adversary has made them. They die just like any other animal, and yet part of them goes on." He paused. "It is as if part of them is like us."

The Master closed his eyes in quiet exasperation. "We have been through this before," he said, revealing his irritation. "As long as that part finds its way down here, and it always does, they can never be gods like us. They are monkeys with ghosts. That's all."

The Guardian bowed.

"Of course, my Lord."

"These vermin spend their miserable lives in fear. They're always digging, scratching for something. Nothing. They live like animals. They die like animals." A crooked grin came to the Master's face. "And they play our games."

"Indeed. It is amazing what they won't do for wealth or power or fame," the Guardian mused, hoping to sound intelligent.

"Forget about wealth and power," the Master corrected. "It's amazing what they won't do for a little extra food or water. The things they can do to one another are" he paused, his silver eyes narrowing, "magnificent."

"Exactly, Master."

He looked down on the blinded and defeated captives, reading their faces. He especially liked the faces revealing terror sharper than death pangs, despair heavier than a sepulcher door. A newly arrived Briton wept endlessly, not daring to open his eyes to the void around him. Next to him stood an old Huecha woman still as a statue, beaten by merciless centuries of blindness. The Master's thin lips parted in ecstasy. A splendid collection growing by the minute. All of it the work of his hands. He swelled with pride. What could the Adversary possibly do to him now? For every obstacle the

Adversary hurled at him, he found a way around it. There was no trickery he could not detect, no treachery he could not strike down by his insurmountable strength. If nothing else, he jokingly thought, he was at least adaptable. But he was far more than that. He remembered what hardships and indignities had led him to his current path. He remembered them well.

☐

His strategy was complete. After countless ages of planning, the Master was finally ready to mount another assault upon the Adversary. The final assault. Doubtlessly, it was complicated. But he knew the Others were devoted to the cause. They would execute his will precisely and fiercely. Nothing would stop him. Hordes of angels would crumble beneath his fury. The Adversary himself would cower and worship at the Master's glorious wrath. He would have no mercy.

Contemplating these things as he walked slowly through an arid wilderness, the Master was struck by the sight of a dense grove of tropical trees. He knew every inch of this particular tract of wilderness and could say with absolute certainty that these trees had not been there before. Over the ages, land masses had shifted, forests had grown and died, ice had buried the earth and melted, of course. But this was different. The trees were far too uniform. There were places on the trunks where branches had been removed cleanly and smoothly, leaving behind no jagged or uneven edges. Even stranger was the complete lack of dead branches on the ground. An eerie calm emanated from the center of this place. He was disturbed, but he needed to understand it. After all, there was a war to win.

Lightly, he stepped into the trees. He dared not leap. This could be a trap. The emerald grove was filled with the usual pestilences. Insects, mammals, and reptiles. Nothing new. Nothing threatening.

But then he heard it.

He froze mid-step. Silence. A distant dragonfly's humming wings. A few more apprehensive steps. He heard it again. Voices. But unnatural voices. He followed the unnerving sound to a small clearing. Light. He had seen that light before. And that is where he saw them.

"If we keep picking this many oranges, we are going to need a bigger basket," said one.

"We can make another one the same size, and I can carry it," said the other.

The Master's eyes widened. They were hideous. Two-legged creatures. A male. A female. Like apes. But not. Smooth. Disgusting. Their sleek dark bodies the color of rich soil. The Master listened to them speak. He understood them perfectly. They reasoned with one another. They laughed. These animals spoke like him. But more like the Adversary.

It was unbelievable.

He panicked. His mind raced at the possibilities. An animal was not like a god; an animal could grow into something stronger, something greater than it was at birth. Gods, on the other hand, never changed. If these animals could reason, he thought, then the Adversary probably intended them to live for eternity. They could grow into something *greater* than gods. Animals with flesh and blood. Growing, but never dying.

How sickening.

There was no word to express the audacity of this kind of insult. This degradation. This abject humiliation. The Master leaped back into the wilderness. A lonesome elk was peacefully grazing on some tall grass. Spotting it, the Master sank his teeth into the beast's neck and plunged his hands into its abdomen, ripping out its throat in a red spray and yanking out its hot entrails into the dirt. With wide eyes, it convulsed at his feet.

He screamed at the heavens, baring his bloodied teeth. The sound reverberated off of nearby mountains with murderous ferocity.

The Elder and several of the Others appeared around him. He grabbed his white head with both dark red hands.

"All hail!" he shouted.

The entire ranks of the Others swarmed, surrounding him.

"Hail, Lord!" they shouted in unison.

"All hail!" he screamed, bloody handprints painting his head, a glistening beard of red smeared across his livid face.

"Hail, Lord!" they shouted again.

He surveyed the legions of pale faced devotees staring earnestly at him with golden eyes. His rage radiated before he spoke a word. It was infectious and sweet. They wanted more.

"My brothers!" he announced. "The strike is off! There has been a new development. We cannot risk our forces, especially since it seems that the Adversary may well be anticipating our campaign."

A fevered murmur surged through the ranks.

"Our enemy" he paused, reeling, "sought to injure us when he expelled us from his presence. Truth be told, this was no injury at all. But now," he scowled savagely, blood dripping from his mouth and hands, "he insults us in the most perverse manner possible…" He ground his red teeth, clenching his blood-bathed hands. "…by putting his stamp on animals!"

Confusion rippled among the Others.

"His *stamp*, my Lord?" asked the Elder.

"They can become like him!" he snarled. "Gruesome hairless beasts that sweat and shit! They speak! They reason!" His voice left him, his crimson mouth open in horror.

No one dared to speak. The air was perfectly still. The Master composed himself in the sight of innumerable puzzled golden eyes.

"He imagines that he can make them greater than us. He is altogether deceived."

Anxious silence.

"I shall tend to this matter personally," he announced. "Await my further instructions."

He vanished, leaving behind only the blood from his hands and head.

+++

Lucifer rejoiced for the gift of his creation. The intensity of his gratitude welled up within him, overflowing. Words seemed far too weak to express the magnitude of his thankfulness. Enraptured, he pondered deeply:

I was not. And now I am.

The solution arose within him. He raised his voice, uttering words of sublime praise to his creator. And yet, they were not merely words. They varied in tone and pitch, creating melody. The sound carried across the heavens above and below, ethereal and pregnant with the deepest yearning. Lucifer knew that his creator, whose light clothed him and bore him up high in the heavens, was the Lord and God of all things, and that there was none like him.

There were, however, others like Lucifer. They, too, were clothed with the light. They differed according to form and shape but not according to magnificence. Taken with Lucifer's song, which expressed their own longing, they joined in, making it their own. According to their gifts, they added to the song, creating harmonies. The heavens resounded with songs of deeply felt praise and thanksgiving as the light of God surrounded and blessed them all.

The sound filled Lucifer's ears. He paused, listening to the melody and harmonies of his fellows. Such beauty. Such sweetness. And he had started it.

+++

Stars adorned the cloudless night sky like so many luminous diamonds spread across royal velvet. Moonlight bathed Rome, reflecting off of limestone and marble, setting the city aglow with its gentle but spectral light. The city slept. All was still and silent. Even asleep, the Coliseum lay majestically triumphant, a never-sleeping testimony to the greatness of Caesar. Deep within the arena, on the glistening moonlit sand, stood the Master. Waiting.

Seventeen gladiators perished here during the day. He had seen them earlier, stumbling through the darkness of the Keep. For one reason or another, their terrified expressions made him laugh, which did not happen often. The fight in the arena had even made him chuckle. Something in the way one of them was choking on his own blood, his wide eyes pleading for mercy as his opponent's blade took his head off. The sand of the arena showed no evidence that they had ever been here. No footprints. No blood. Nothing. The scores of people who had earlier stood in the seats sweating and shouting for the gladiators' blood would not remember them either. They were gone forever. Sand blown away. The Master laughed again, remembering their faces.

Finally, the Elder arrived beside him.

"That took long enough," the Master said coldly.

"Begging your pardon, my Lord, but I had to be sure." The Elder bowed reverently.

"What did you find?" he asked piercingly.

Straightening himself, the Elder began earnestly, "This Aberration we have been hearing about from the Others, it is exactly as they have said."

"Yes?"

"He never gives in. Nothing works on him. The best Voices we have all say that he never bends to their suggestions."

"Not now, at any rate," interjected the Master. "How far back does this go?"

"That is where we are lost, Master." The Elder paused, looking down, not wanting to proceed. "No one knows." He raised his eyes to the Master. "There are gaps in the reports about him."

"Gaps?" The Master frowned, staring at the Elder, taking slow steps toward him. Shadows grew in his furrowed brow, sharpening his features.

"This lack of vigilance among our ranks is aggravating, to say the least. One would think that our forces would keep a sharp eye fixed on such an anomaly."

He restrained his anger and kicked the sand softly, turning his face toward the moon, its pale light reflecting off of his face and eyes.

Reflectively, he continued, "We have dealt with similar cases before, although not identical. None of those ultimately posed any threat to us." He laughed. "When have any of these piss-ants ever been a problem?"

"Of course, my Lord. Even the Adversary's most devoted of followers always end up in the Keep."

The Master shook his head in agreement, still smiling smugly.

"In the meantime, keep a team on him at all times. Have them study his habits. Eventually, they should be able to find the cracks in him. Find the cracks, stick in your claws, and break him to pieces. He will die, they all do, so that's not a problem. But if we can hollow him out first, leaving him with nothing inside, we make him our plaything. To enjoy and to discard."

"As you wish, Master," he said, bowing. "Will there be anything else?"

"For future reference," the Master began, "where is he from?"

"Judea. Nazareth, as far as we can tell."

The Master smirked.

"Nazareth is a dunghill. You can't see the humans for the flies."

The Elder gave a low chuckle.

"His name, Ba'al?"

"Jesus, son of Joseph, my Lord."

"Jesus," the Master repeated. "I look forward to seeing the look on his face, if I'm not busy, that is."

"The look, my Lord?"

"When they feel the horror of the emptiness inside them and they want nothing more than to die," he explained with pleasant enthusiasm. "That look."

+

John the Baptist was a menace. The Master had been informed that Herod's soldiers would arrest him on the first day of the week. Although it would be a while before John actually met his end, the Master wanted to witness the arrest just to tide him over.

The day was hot and cloudless. Hundreds of people swarmed at the banks of the Jordan River. Sweating and crying and seeking deliverance. The Baptist was dedicated, the Master admitted, which made him annoying. Whores, gangsters, tax collectors, adulterers, drunkards, and even Roman soldiers flocked to him daily asking to be washed clean of their sins, wanting to change the direction of their lives and live only for God. As if it mattered. The honest man and the murderer were equals in death.

There he was. His lean, tan body wrapped in camel skin. His matted black beard and hair reaching his waist. His piercing brown eyes burning with zeal, but not fanaticism. Zeal tempered and grounded by profound wisdom. Which made him no fun at all.

The Master stood atop a hillside fifty yards from the bank, watching the Baptist wade through the aqua-green water to the penitents weeping before him. A group of tax collectors came out to him with long faces, disregarding their fine linen clothes as they trudged toward him through the water.

"Rabbi," began the youngest one, a wisp of downy beard on his chin. "What should we do?"

"Take no more than what is appointed to you," John replied.

"Pray for us, please," he cried.

John submerged each of them, blessing them, "May the Lord grant you strength."

For six solid hours, the Master stood still, watching. If nothing else, he was at least patient, he thought, but this grew tiresome. Where were Herod's soldiers? A tiny gray lizard scuttled along a few inches from the Master's feet. He crushed it and kicked it down the hill. What was taking so long?

The Elder appeared at his side.

"Still no Herod?"

"No."

"I am sure his men will be here."

The Master said nothing. He stared flatly at John with arms crossed. One after another, the Baptist gave counsel to and dunked another creature. And another. This was tedious.

A young man of thirty waded into the water. Tan skin. Black hair and beard. Rough hands and clothes. Like so many others. Unlike the others, his face was not drawn in an expression of sorrow or plaintiveness. He was perfectly calm. He waited for his turn to speak with the Baptist. When they came face to face, John froze, his eyes and mouth open in wonder. Neither spoke. The Master leaped closer. This was odd.

John spoke shakily, "It is I who need to be baptized by you, and you come to me?"

The Elder leaped beside the Master.

"My Lord, this…"

"Shut up, damn it!"

The young man replied, "Allow it to be so for now. We must fulfill all righteousness."

The Baptist took him by the shoulders and pressed him down into the water.

He arose.

A rushing wind whipped through the crowd, rustling branches, stirring up dust.

The voice, surpassing majesty and bearing peace, came down to them.

"This is my beloved Son in whom I am well pleased. Listen to him."

The crowd stirred with excitement, pleasantly bewildered. Did the voice come from heaven? Was it the voice of God? Was it a voice at all? Who is the "beloved Son" the voice spoke of? That man who was just baptized? No, it wasn't a voice, it was thunder. No, it was a voice. Thunder. A voice. Whose voice? A voice.

The Master and the Elder both recognized that voice. Their brows hardened with trepidation.

As they watched, something came down from the sky upon the young man. Like the voice. They could not quite make out its shape. Something like a dove. Whatever it was, it seemed to rest on him visibly, and yet invisibly.

His mouth agape, the Master managed to utter, "My *Son*? What does that mean?" He broke off, his mind reeling. "Since when has the Adversary had a son? This is just a man…"

Their eyes were fixed on him as he waded through the water. The Elder's expression revealed a deeper terror than the Master's.

"My Lord, that…young man…"

"What?"

"…he…"

"What about him, God damn it?!" the Master snapped, turning sharply to the Elder.

"He is the Aberration…he is the one…" he stammered.

Torrents of possibilities flooded the Master's mind, drowning him, leaving him gasping for answers and finding none. Gasping and drowning. A son? What does that mean? Did you ever see a son? For that matter, did you ever actually see *him* behind the light? Can't remember. Can't. Pacing and mumbling, the Master struggled to put the pieces together. He stopped, putting his fingers to his temples, looking down. After a minute, he straightened.

He tracked the Aberration wading through the water. The young man moved his hair out of his eyes and sneezed.

"This does not look good, Ba'al. This...I can't...," he stopped. "I have to figure this out. Myself."

They watched the young man climb the opposite bank. His clothes and hair heavy with water, he headed toward the wilderness calm as he was before.

The Master faced the Elder, taking him by the shoulders.

"You are first in command until I return. I don't know when that will be. Do not disappoint me," he trailed off. "You will all know when it is finished."

"As you wish. Hail, Lord!" The Elder bowed and was gone.

Turning back to the Aberration, the Master followed him silently into the wilderness.

+

What a strange man. For forty days the Master hounded his steps through the hot Palestinian wilderness, saying nothing. Watching for something, anything, that might give him a clue as to who Jesus was.

The Aberration prayed intensely throughout the day and into much of the night. He ate nothing. For all the solitude and silence, he did not appear to be disturbed by anything. Heat, insects, dust, hunger, or thirst. He felt them all and accepted them. Prayer sustained him. It was his food, his drink, his breath in the heart of the parched wilderness. Peace surrounded him. It emanated from him.

By contrast, the Master found the silence oppressive. It smothered him, crippling him with anxiety. He felt he would have to scream out just for a little relief, but he did not want to alert the Aberration as to his presence. The scream writhed cruelly within him, pulling and tearing. This must be what disembowelment feels like, he thought. Tracking a victim never bothered him before, so why now? It was unbearable. The Master could not feel hunger, the heat of the sun, or physical exhaustion, yet tedium clung to him like burning pitch. This talking monkey, on the other hand, would not lash out or give any visible sign that this accursed wilderness bothered him at all. It was insufferable.

On the forty-first day, the Master noticed Jesus heading slowly toward civilization. Finally. His steps were somewhat shaky but determined. He had to stop several times to maintain his balance and to keep from fainting. This rather intense fast was obviously meant to prepare him for something great. And now it was over. Jesus walked on, weak with hunger.

It was time to make him crack. Right now. The Others had failed, but the Master would succeed.

Jesus stopped again, kneeling this time among the stones and scattered grasses. He was starving. The Master had seen it before. His foul mood took a sharp turn, and now he tingled with excitement. The tyranny of this creature's belly would bend him to the Master's will. Through the millennia, men had sold their own children into slavery, and worse, just to alleviate their own hunger pains. However, the Master reflected, one must also understand the importance of false pretense — the real value of hypocrisy. There was nothing destructive about being hungry. What ruined these animals is what they did when they were hungry. What made them even worse is how they justified what they did. The Aberration could claim that he was demonstrating that he was the Son of God, when he was really just giving in to the dictates of his body.

Like creeping mist, the Master appeared beside him, making himself visible. Their eyes met. Jesus's face was deeply weathered, tan, and peppered with dirt. An artificial smile haunted the Master's lips. He stooped, picking up two large brown stones with his white hands.

"If you are the Son of God," he said softly, "command these stones to become bread."

Now, take the bait.

Jesus stood, continuing to look him in the eyes. A slight breeze tousled his dirty black hair.

"It is written," he began, "'Man does not live by bread alone but by every word that proceeds out of the mouth of God.'"

He walked away from the Master, not looking back.

Astounded, the Master watched him walk away. That wasn't supposed to happen. They were supposed to have a dialogue, maybe even a little debate. The Master was supposed to persuade him if he should raise any objections. Just like that, the Aberration cut him off. This man was truly in control of his passions. How utterly bizarre. Not even starvation could tip him to the breaking point. The Master had not asked him to kill anybody to satisfy his hunger, just to turn rocks into bread. But he would not do it. Not for the Master. Disappointing. But not disheartening.

Scripture was the answer.

The Aberration fancied himself an expert on Scripture. What he probably did not realize was that no one knew Scripture better than the Master. In some ways, it was one of the Master's favorite weapons. He took great delight in bending the Adversary's words into a sword to slice, a boulder to crush, a fire to burn. What glorious irony, he often thought, using the Adversary's book against him and his creatures.

Only a man of great faith could fast for forty days and refuse the Master's request, citing Scripture. But even great faith could lead to great pride. Again, hypocrisy was the answer. A little hypocrisy covered a multitude of virtues. The Aberration could perform some leap of faith, claiming to demonstrate the greatness of his God, when really he would be demonstrating the greatness of his own faith. And with great faith, he could sink and drown in his great pride.

The Master caught up with him and took him by the wrist, leaping through the wilderness and the city to the pinnacle of the Temple at Jerusalem. Oddly, the Aberration did not seem surprised. Placing his hand on Jesus's shoulder, the Master waited a moment to allow him to see the great height at which they stood. Hopefully dizziness would set in.

"If you are the Son of God, cast yourself down, for it is written, *'He shall give his angels charge over you,'* and, *'in their hands shall they bear you up, lest at any time you should dash your foot against a stone.'"*

This *will* work.

Jesus turned to him, neither dizzy nor afraid.

"Again, it is written, *'You shall not tempt the Lord your God.'"*

He turned, looking for a safe way down to the ground below.

What was this? Who was this man? Didn't he want to make a name for himself among religious people? Didn't he want to be admired by thousands for his devotion to God? Didn't he want to be revered as the Great Rabbi whose faith was unmatched even by Moses and the prophets? This pious little ape refused to make a show of his faith. He had nothing to prove to the Master. Nothing. He was positively incorruptible. Or was he?

The Master panicked.

Again, he grabbed Jesus by the wrist and leaped to the top of a high mountain. Beneath them, the great kingdoms of the earth floated by as on a stream. Rome. Persia. China. Ethiopia. On and on they flowed, the glory of their opulent palaces ablaze with color. The wealth of their cities reflected in masterfully crafted buildings and streets. Kings and queens dressed in fine linens, silks, and brocades sat luxuriously on gilt litters carried by slaves. Treasury rooms a hundred feet tall held mountains of gold and fine jewels touching the ceiling. Banquet tables fifty yards long creaked beneath the weight of the finest delicacies. The perfumed air of harems led to warmly lit rooms full of shapely women. Anything and everything a man could want.

Stepping upon a small boulder, the Master looked earnestly down on the Aberration. This had to work. No man in his right mind could refuse this. Jesus looked up at him as the kingdoms passed by in splendor.

"All of these things," the Master started, "I will give to you if you will just bow down and worship me."

Power. Fame. Wealth. Sex. Comfort. Limitlessly.

Jesus did not hesitate.

He jumped upon the boulder and looked down into the Master's silver eyes.

"Get behind me, Satan!" he shouted, his voice echoing off the mountain.

The sound rebounded loudly, *Satan!...Satan!...Satan!*

"It is written, *'You shall worship the Lord your God, and him only shall you serve!'"*

The Master stepped back as if by reflex, compelled by fear. There was something in the

Aberration's voice which disturbed him. It had always been there, but he just now became keenly aware of it. It was the same eerie quality the Master felt simply by being in the Aberration's presence. Purest hatred lit the Master's face as he stared into Jesus's determined brown eyes. Opening his mouth slightly, as if to speak, the Master remained silent. It is already over for you, he thought. His mouth pulled into a weak smile, his cold eyes animated with eons of murders, rapes, betrayals, and unimaginable degradations. What would be suitable for this little ape?

The Aberration had made his choice. And he chose death. A gruesome death.

Leaving Jesus alone on the mountain, the Master had work to do.

+

Speculating and murmuring atop a high mesa in the land of the Navajo, the Council waited. Dusk set the sky aglow with molten orange, fading to lavenders and deeper purples. Mesas and pillars of rock stood painted in strata of burnt browns, oranges, beiges, and yellows. Cracked red earth lay punctuated by black shadows growing longer and longer. The Council cast no shadows.

"Did he say what it was about?" asked Moloch.

"He only said to be here at sunset," replied the Elder.

"No doubt it has to do with the Aberration," quipped a tall, broad shouldered Voice.

"I, for one, hope we're getting new assignments. The Baptist is really shitting on our work in Palestine."

The Master arrived, his back to the dying sun.

Forming two columns, the Council saluted in unison.

"Hail, Lord!"

They stood rigidly at attention as he walked slowly in their midst, hands clasped behind his back. He said nothing. Reaching the end of their ranks, he turned to face the last fierce traces of the setting sun, the silver of his eyes reflecting ember red.

"Brothers, we have a problem."

The Council waited with concerned faces. Rarely did the Master call them together.

"His name," he continued with a sneer, "is Jesus of Nazareth. The Aberration. The one whom the Adversary has called 'Son.'"

He watched the sun disappear beneath the rocky horizon.

"This man is incorruptible. There is no way any of our usual methods will break him. He has perfect mastery over his body. He is not prideful. And he cares nothing about power. Obviously, he is a tool of the Adversary. I am certain that he is the promised Messiah written about by those miserable prophets."

Moloch spoke first.

"My Lord, this is certainly distressing, but it also seems that the solution is fairly simple. If we can't corrupt him, let's just kill him and be done with it. Granted, it won't be as satisfying, since he won't crack, but at least it's something."

"We will kill him, Moloch," the Master began, petulantly, "but not now. The Adversary has invested a great deal in him. He is to be a leader for the 'chosen people,' a symbol of righteousness. We can't hollow him out. If *I* can't do it, then it positively can't be done. But we can hollow out those around him and those who will look up to him."

The Elder gave a knowing, crooked smile.

"Exalt him in the eyes and hearts of the people, then crush him," he beamed.

"Precisely, Ba'al," nodded the Master. "There is a world of difference between reality and perception. He is the Adversary's 'Holy One' — the Messiah. The people will believe that. But what *is* a Messiah? What does a Messiah look like? How does a Messiah behave? What should a Messiah do?" He placed his pale hands on his chest. "*I* decide that."

He paused, watching the purple sky give way to cerulean and stars.

"The prophets said that he will open the eyes of the blind." His mouth pulled into a wide smile, revealing his teeth. "If he does, we must control *what* they see. And *how* they see it."

The Council nodded approvingly.

He raised a prophetic hand, projecting his words as images upon the night sky.

"The people will rejoice at the long awaited arrival of their deliverer. They will marvel at his

great works. They will follow him wherever he goes,   ·
hanging on his every word. They will burn with
fiery zeal, ready to follow him to the ends of the
earth, ready to usher in the new age at the point of
the sword. And when he disappoints them and their
hearts sink," he grinned, "they will cut him to pieces
and leave him for the vultures."

Coyotes howled faintly in the distance.

"How should we proceed, Lord?" asked the
broad shouldered Voice.

"Naturally, there will be people who get close
to him and people who hate him, Asmodeus," the
Master started. "Exploit their weaknesses. Uncover
their motivations. What drives them? What do they
want? What do they fear? How can we pit them
against one another?"

Raising his chin, the Master spread his arms
widely to the Council, as if embracing them.

"You all are my chosen ones. You have proven
yourselves most loyal and efficient in the long ages
we have been together. There is none I would
entrust this great task to other than you. Now,
understand that I will be working with you closely.
This urgent matter requires *my* attention and *our*
intimate collaboration and communication. I will not
tolerate failure from anyone. For *any* reason."

His arms fell to his side.

"The prophets of the Adversary, those pathetic,
sad bastards…no one listened to them when they
were alive. We saw to that. And now, no one
remembers them."

Of one accord, the Council laughed.

"How exquisite it will be ages and ages from now when no one remembers the failed mission of the failed Messiah, Jesus of Nazareth!"

+++

The Lord called them by name, giving each a task. Word began to spread that they were each to receive a commission to fulfill. Each waited with joyful expectation for his assignment. Lucifer and those next to him waited silently. They watched and listened as one was called. And another. And another. With each being called and sent, Lucifer began to sense the smallest bit of disquiet within himself. Why were so many receiving their commissions before him? When would the Lord get to him? What would the Lord give to him? He had no way of knowing. Soon, disquiet became anxiety.

More names and more commissions. More waiting. Perhaps there was nothing for Lucifer to do, or perhaps it was something menial. After what seemed like eternity passed, the Lord spoke to Lucifer and those around him.

"My beloved Lucifer, Michael, Gabriel, Raphael, Uriel, Selaphiel, Yegoudiel, and Varachiel," he began. Lucifer held perfectly still. "You are the Archangels, the commanders of all the heavenly hosts. It falls to you to direct the others."

Relief. And satisfaction. How silly it was for him to worry. The Lord had intended him to work in the highest capacity all along. Now he could show the Lord just what he could do. He could prove his worth. Who could know what fantastic things Lucifer could do for the Lord?

41

+++

"Blessed are the poor in spirit, for theirs is the kingdom of heaven. Blessed are they that mourn, for they shall be comforted.   Blessed are the meek, for they shall inherit the earth. Blessed are they that hunger and thirst after righteousness, for they shall be filled…"

Low gray clouds hung close to the mountain upon which the Aberration stood. His closest followers and thousands of curious spectators of all walks of life surrounded him as an army of moths drawn to a strange new flame. The air was light and cool despite the low cloud cover. Rapt in his words, many of the people listened as if life depended upon it. Time disappeared. Never had a man spoken like this. Not even among scribes, lawyers, and Pharisees, some of whom were there. There was something different about him.

Hanging at the edge of the crowd near the foot of the mountain, the Master and the Council watched and listened sharply.

"…And when you pray, do not be as the hypocrites, for they love to pray standing in the synagogues and in the corners of the streets that they may be seen by men. I tell you, truly, they have their reward…"

The Council read the faces of the crowd as he spoke. Remorse. Amusement. Zeal. Resentment. Desperation. Detachment. Hunger. Encouragement.

An elderly woman listened with tears standing on the edge of her leathery eyelids, coursing down her creased, lean face. Was he the promised Messiah that Judea has waited for?

A young scribe with a patchy beard scowled disapprovingly, his arms crossed with indignation. Who the hell did this rabbi think he was?

A well-dressed middle-aged Zealot, his hands accustomed to violence and itching to shed Roman blood, studied him skeptically. Could this idealistic young rabbi serve as a tool in the struggle to rid Judea of Roman oppression and Herodian corruption?

Hope. Scheming. Uncertainty. Offended sensibilities. Each face revealed a reaction for the Master and the Council to exploit.

"...For if you forgive men their trespasses, your heavenly Father will also forgive you. But if you do not forgive men their trespasses, neither will your Father forgive your trespasses..."

How odd.

This was the Messiah. But he was asking the people to forgive those who sinned against them. To forgive. Even the Romans. If he truly was the Messiah, he certainly had no interest in spilling Roman blood or anyone else's. How would he establish a kingdom, then? Wasn't that the Adversary's plan? To set up his kingdom on earth? Turning the problem over and over, the Master almost frowned.

He found the answer.

A *political* Messiah. The Master was expecting the Messiah to be a man of the sword. Doubtlessly, the people were expecting the same. It appeared as though the Adversary was planning something different.

The sermon ended.

Jesus walked slowly down the mountain, the multitudes pressing in on him. Those closest to him glowed with joyful expectation. This man was different. This man had real authority. This man had been touched by the Lord God himself. This man was the answer to prayers.

A young man wrapped in white from head to foot walked toward the Aberration. Noticing him, people recoiled in fear, not wanting to be contaminated.

"Unclean!" the young man shouted periodically. "Unclean!"

People scattered as insects from a fire.

Approaching Jesus, he stopped. The Aberration looked at the young man compassionately. The sullied white cloth wrapped around his head revealed only his eyes. Leprosy had eaten the right side of his face completely and was creeping to the left. He bowed before Jesus on his knees.

"Lord," he began tremulously, looking to the ground, "if you will, you can make me clean."

The onlookers froze aghast as the Aberration stepped closer to the young leper.

"No, Master!" shouted a faceless voice.

He stretched out his tan calloused hand and touched the leper on the face. More gasps and murmuring.

"I will. Be clean."

Removing his hand, the people could see that the bloated dead white flesh of leprosy was gone from the young man's face. The young man removed the cloth from his face and head with a bandaged hand. He tore the bandages off of his hands. His smooth olive skin was restored. Amazement shone from the faces of those who witnessed it. Excited voices spread the news to those who couldn't see.

Jesus spoke quietly.

"See that you tell no man, but go your way, show yourself to the priest, and offer the gift that Moses commanded for a testimony to them."

The young man bowed again with tears in his almond eyes. He said nothing but rose and walked away.

"A healer, too," the Master muttered.

Asmodeus scowled.

"He just healed that rotting creature in full view of everyone. What does he mean, 'See that you tell no man'?" he asked.

The Master and the Council followed the Aberration toward the road with the crowd.

"Our little Messiah doesn't care about fame," said the Master, dryly. "But he does put on quite a show. Word of this is spreading already. Like leprosy. Soon, all of Judea will be infected with hope."

The Elder's knitted brow tightened.

"What can we do about it, Lord? We can't exactly reverse the work of the Adversary."

Watching the Aberration go further down the road to Capernaum, the Master stopped for a moment. The Council turned to him, waiting for an answer.

"We can't reverse it. We don't need to. But we can control how these beasts understand it. Let him perform his magic tricks. Let the crowds cheer and holler. To those who are interested in healing, let him be a faith healer. But nothing *more*. To those who are expecting a warrior Messiah who will stick Roman heads on spikes throughout Judea, make him out to be a warrior. And nothing *less*."

Turning back toward the road, the Master confidently resumed his stride, and the Council followed. The pieces were moving.

+

Violent wind battered the side of the boat and its terrified passengers. The frenzied men clung desperately to life, pulling ropes with calloused and blistered hands, shouting with hoarse voices against the deafening roar of the cutting wind, soaked and beaten by the waves that rose to devour their small vessel. Rain and stinging sea spray blinded them. Darkness yawned to swallow them whole.

In the turbulence above, the Master and the Council encircled the small ship tossed about to the point of splitting to splinters. Looking down, the

Master watched without expression as the helpless men scrambled about to stay alive.

"Andrew, let down the sail! The mast is going to snap!" shouted the bulky one from the prow.

A crushing wave from the starboard side almost blasted him out of the boat. He hung over the edge by one muscular arm. Straining, grunting, he pulled himself quickly back onto the deck.

"This one is a born leader, but he acts before he thinks," the Master shouted through the thunder, addressing the Council.

The wind and rain did not touch them. A flash of lightning illuminated their piercing eyes in the green darkness.

"Peter!" screamed his brother, abandoning the sail and rushing to his side.

"This one has a bit more discretion," commented the Elder. "But not by much."

Two slender brothers directed the others to cast any and all cargo overboard.

"Who are these two, Master?" asked Asmodeus.

"James and John," he replied.

Asmodeus nodded his head.

"They seem capable," he quipped.

The brothers shouted almost in unison.

"Ropes! Bags! Everything!"

Furiously, the other men threw out anything they could grab.

A short man quickly snatched up a leather pouch, securing it tightly beneath his tunic.

The Master smiled crookedly, laughing.

"Can't part with the money, can you, Judas?" His silver eyes narrowed. "You will be useful."

An endless barrage of waves threatened to overturn the weak vessel. It could not take much more. Evenly distributing their weight across the boat, the frightened men fought to keep it from capsizing.

Of course, one man would be sleeping.

"Lord, save us!" Peter shouted. He stooped and shook the Aberration by the shoulders from his sleep. "We are going to die!"

How irritating, the Master thought. Not even a massive sea storm could stir this peaceful little Messiah from his peaceful little sleep. Look at him. His beard and hair are soaked, and he's just now shaking off the drowsiness. Not from apathy, mind you, but from the blessed peace of the blessed Adversary. Bastard...

The Master's eye twitched.

Rising to his feet, his clothes rapidly saturated by the rain and spray, the Aberration spoke sternly.

"Why are you fearful, you of little faith?"

His tone was admonishing, not accusing.

He shouted something the Master could not understand into the maelstrom thrashing and whipping around them.

Silence and calm strangled the wind and the waves with mighty hands.

The storm died.

Jesus stood dripping in the midst of his companions, the Master, and the Council. He pressed his hands to his hair and beard, wringing out the water. His companions stared at him, marveling. He walked back to his corner and lay down.

The Council was ill at ease. The Master remained stoically unmoved.

"Master," Moloch whispered nervously, "he can make the elements obey him."

"He can also heal all manner of diseases, Moloch. Don't forget that." He smirked.

Moloch eyed the Master incredulously, speechless.

Condescending to the Council's anxiety, the Master rounded on them.

"Forget about miracles. These maggots will. Their heart-felt gratitude and wide-eyed amazement will die. Soon. All of the wonders he performs for them will soon have the all the appeal of a filthy old menstrual rag."

Slowly, the Council began to understand.

"Tonight, he saved their lives. Tomorrow, they would gladly return the favor. A year from now when the dynamics in the group have changed and danger is upon them, don't count on it. These animals will have no memory of past blessings when faced with imminent death. We have seen it before with the 'chosen people' ages ago. Moses managed to lead them out of slavery in Egypt. The Adversary sustained them in the wilderness, giving them food and water. Everything they needed. And what did they do? They bitched about the food, about Moses, about everything. They wanted to go back to Egypt! To slavery!"

He turned to watch the boat move peacefully through the night. The Aberration was already back to sleep. His friends stared at him as he snored. They exchanged astonished glances with each other.

Peter stepped closer to him.

"What kind of man is this that even the winds and the sea obey him?"

The Master sneered.

"The kind who's going to get you and your friends killed, Peter."

+

Tracking the Aberration and his disciples became almost exhilarating. At first, the Council approached the task with fear and uncertainty. Indeed, the legions of Others remained petrified at the mere mention of the Aberration, the Son of God. The Master's inspiring guidance, however, filled the Council with courage, leading them to fight this new battle with teeth and claws poised to strike. Each moment was an undiscovered country ready to be conquered.

The Aberration's ship touched the shore of the Gadarenes next to Galilee. Relieved to see daylight and land again, the disciples got out of the boat and pulled it ashore with palpable gratitude, soaking the sunlight into their weather beaten faces, drinking in the cool morning air. On the shaded side of a nearby mountain, herds upon herds of pigs grazed in peace, the faint din of their grunts adding a pleasant note to the perfect calm of the morning.

Peter laughed.

"I never thought I would be so happy to see pigs again."

They all smiled. James and Judas laughed in agreement.

The Council and the Master touched down on the shore, watching.

"We have Tormentors at work in this town, don't we?" asked the Elder.

"We do," answered the Master. "Unfortunately, they are still afraid of the Aberration."

The Elder laughed, masking his anxiety.

A single wide road started about seventy yards from the shore, and Jesus led the way toward it. They had barely reached it when an inhuman scream split the tranquil air, attacking their ears. It was the sound of a hundred livid voices straining to screech through a single blistered throat. Bottomless hatred. A moaning wail followed, full of abysmal misery, expressing the desire to die and the inability to do so.

He appeared from a grove of trees. Naked. Covered in scrapes, cuts, sores, and dirt. Broken manacles hanging from his bruised skeletal wrists. Patches of hair pulled out all over his head. Black blood and hair caked under his monstrous fingernails. His wide, bloodshot eyes wild with hatred and fear. He ran, stumbled, crawled, stumbled, ran, stumbled, crawled, crawled, stumbled, crawled toward Jesus. The disciples recoiled in disgusted shock. He stunk of feces even from a distance. Halting on his knees ten feet from Jesus, he writhed, convulsed, and dug his nails into his chest, his mouth open wide, revealing browned and blackened teeth.

Digging his nails into his scalp, not daring to raise his eyes, he screamed, "What have I to do with you, Jesus, you Son of the most high God?" Growling, he gasped, "I beg you, do not torment me!"

He hammered on his head with both fists and scratched new raw lines into his emaciated face. Jesus took a step toward him. He scuttled backward like a crab, breathing rapidly, the lines in his face starting to bleed.

"What is your name?" the Aberration asked.

His jaw hanging open, he gave a guttural growl before answering.

"Legion!" he hissed. "Please!" he grunted, "Please! Do not cast us into the abyss! Not yet! Not yet!" He wept bitterly and tearlessly, howling.

Shaking his head in disappointment, the Master muttered inaudibly, "Only the Adversary could do that, you miserable cowards."

The disciples looked on, horrified. Never had they seen a man so utterly wasted or so fearfully savage.

Pressing his face to the ground, the man shouted again.

"The pigs! Please! Let us go into the pigs! Please! Not the abyss! Not now! Not now!"

Jesus raised his voice, "Go, then."

Trying to laugh at the idiocy of his Tormentors, the Master once again felt irked by the hideous quality of the Aberration's voice.

The poor man convulsed violently and lay still on his face, perfectly motionless.

On the mountainside, the pigs' pleasant grunting turned into a cacophony of tortured squeals. The swineherds at the top of the mountain went stiff with alarm. A few of them caught a glance of Jesus on the road below, standing only a foot from the man they knew. *That* man. The one full of demons. The one who lived in the tombs and would beat you within an inch of your life if you got close to him. Rumbling hooves stirred up chalky dust, making the swineherds cough. Of one mind, the pigs tore down the mountain, racing for the sea. By dozens, by fifties, by hundreds, their fat bodies plunged into the water, squealing, crashing, thrashing, drowning. Not one was left.

The storm of noise subsided to a few isolated splashes and gurgling grunts. Then it was quiet. The swineherds who witnessed the source of the disaster dropped their staves and ran toward the town.

Jesus took the man's hand. He raised him to his knees and then to his feet. Dazed gratitude filled his eyes. Without a word, James and John took him to the seaside where he washed himself. Peter went with them, searching the boat for an extra tunic.

Finding one, he gave it to the man when he was done bathing, along with a small damp loaf of bread. The famished man devoured the bread as Peter pried the manacles off his wrists one hand at a time. Returning to the shore, Jesus and the disciples talked with the man as he sat eating another loaf of bread that Peter found.

Half an hour passed as they talked on the sea shore. A large crowd of the city's residents marched down the road to its end by the sea, led by the swineherds.

"There he is," said one of the witnesses, pointing at Jesus.

The crowd followed, marveling at *that* man sitting still, wearing clothes.

"Oh my God," several onlookers muttered.

Fear vibrated among the townsfolk as they looked from the pacified man, to the empty mountainside, and back to the Aberration.

He destroyed your livelihood. How will you eat? What will you do?

The Master smirked triumphantly, looking back at the Elder and Asmodeus plying their talents as Voices. He turned his gaze back to the Aberration.

"That's right, Messiah. Not everyone is interested in what you have to sell."

Relief permeated the air around the Council as they watched the disciples get back into the boat. Only Jesus and the man remained on the shore.

"Please, Lord, let me come with you," he asked almost in desperation.

Jesus smiled warmly and placed his hand on the man's shoulder.

"Return to your own house, and show what great things God has done for you."

Kissing the Aberration's hand with heartfelt reverence, the man bowed and walked toward the road, looking over his shoulder as Jesus climbed into the boat pulling away from shore.

"Good work Ba'al and Asmodeus," the Master praised.

They nodded nervously.

Hailing the attention of the Council, the Master spoke.

"Inform the Others that they have nothing to fear. It would be dreadfully disappointing if this operation were to go up in flames because of their cowardice."

"Certainly, Lord," the Elder responded, forcing a grin.

The Council looked at the ground, clasping their pale hands.

+

The pleasure was short-lived. True, the people of the Gadarenes told the Aberration and his men to get the hell out of their precious pig farming community, but unforeseeable catastrophes awaited. The Aberration healed a paralyzed man in Capernaum, but not before telling him that his sins were forgiven. Trying to heroically seize the moment, the Council whispered to the scribes standing by: *This man blasphemes. Only God can forgive sins.* Their boldness was rudely thwarted. Apparently the Aberration could read hearts and minds, as well. "Why do you think evil in your hearts?" he asked them. Damn. Unsurprisingly, the paralytic soon stood, exulting in his healing.

The Master shrugged it off. So the Aberration could forgive sins. So what? What did God's forgiveness matter, since each of these insects wound up dead, anyway? One major benefit arose from the situation—enmity with the scribes. Their rigidness and political sway could certainly prove useful in the future.

Additionally, things were about to get spiced up. After healing the paralytic, the Aberration passed by the custom house and asked the tax collector to come follow him. He agreed. This posed a problem in terms of appearances. While Judas Iscariot was a thief, he stole secretly, and most people liked him. Nobody liked Matthew the tax collector, because he stole openly from everyone with the blessing of Caesar himself. The tax collector's neighbors often said that pigs were more kosher than him.

Matthew invited the Aberration and the disciples to his house for dinner. Soon, Capernaum buzzed with the news. Puzzlement led to questions. Questions led to gossip. Gossip led to more puzzlement. Matthew the tax collector? That beady-eyed son of a bitch who gets fat off of our hard work? What would that good rabbi have to do with such scum? Indeed, was this rabbi even *allowed* to sit in the house of such a sinner? What did the Law of Moses say? The Voices gladly helped to fan the flames of this little scandal in sleepy little Capernaum.

Jesus and his disciples arrived at Matthew's house first. Naturally, it was the finest house on the street. The people's tax denarii hard at work. Soon after, Matthew's friends and acquaintances showed up. More tax collectors like himself, a few of Capernaum's better known prostitutes, and some well-connected gangsters with their henchmen. Matthew's house became quite the spectacle for passersby. Several of Capernaum's prominent Pharisees had to see it for themselves.

He has no respect for the Law. He eats with whores and criminals.

Most of the Pharisees who passed by looked in, expressed their moral outrage to the other spectators, and went home to their own dinners. However, there were three who were too angry to go home. Their wives and children could wait for them. Waiting outside the despised tax collector's house on the opposite side of the street, the Pharisees looked accusingly at the Aberration, the yellow sun sinking into the west over Capernaum, covering them in shadow.

You recognize that woman. She just brushed up against him.

Finally, the dinner was over. The disciples and the Aberration thanked Matthew for his hospitality and bade farewell to the other guests. Andrew and Judas stepped out first into the cool evening. The youngest of the three Pharisees called across the street to them, his righteous gaze fixed on them with pure zeal.

"Why does your master eat with tax collectors and sinners?"

Because he is a sinner. He cares nothing for the Law of Moses or the customs of our fathers.

Andrew and Judas looked at one another, dumbfounded. More disciples came out into the street.

"Why?" he repeated.

They have no answer, because they are sinners.

Jesus came out last. He crossed the street to the three Pharisees and addressed the young man.

"They who are whole do not need a physician, but they who are sick."

The young Pharisee scowled at him deeply.

Addressing the three, the Aberration spoke with admonition.

"Go, and learn what this means, '*I will have mercy, and not sacrifice.*' I have not come to call the righteous, but sinners to repentance."

Their eyes widened with indignation.

This man who eats with tax collectors, prostitutes, and thugs dares to quote the Scriptures at you who are righteous? For shame! For shame!

Jesus turned to his disciples, and they followed him down the street. The Pharisees watched him with disdain as he shrunk in the distance.

"The nerve of this young upstart lecturing *us*!" rasped the oldest one, his bushy eyebrows giving the appearance of turtledove wings, his puckered mouth disappearing in his beard.

Keep your eye on him. He will be trouble.

"If we didn't have the Law, we would be no better than the Gentiles," remarked the young one. "The Law keeps us holy. If we do not keep the Law, there will be nothing to keep us."

The other two nodded piously.

Warn the brethren about him. He could be a problem.

Parting ways, they departed to their homes, stars emerging over quiet Capernaum.

From the roof of the tax collector's house, the Master watched them for only a moment and turned to the Council. His eyes radiated resolution and confidence.

"Listen to me closely, brothers. We now have enough ammunition to make a coordinated attack. Ba'al and Asmodeus," he announced, "you will follow the religious authorities and their sycophants. Direct the Voices to stir up religious fervor among them. No opportunity is too small or insignificant. These holy little worms are in love with the details of their rules. Puff them up every time they keep one. Blow them up every time the Aberration breaks one. They are the key to his death.

"Moloch and Chemosh, you will follow his disciples and guide Voices accordingly. They all believe that he is the Messiah. The trouble is none of them are sure about what that means. That is what we want. Build up their image of the warrior Messiah. Of course, as always, attack their weaknesses. Peter is impetuous, Judas Iscariot is a thief, and so on. Look for ways to create lines of division among them. When the time is right, we will crush them all. Gloriously.

"The rest of you, tend to the people. You know exactly what to do."

He stopped, crossing his arms, eyeing his elite.

"I will rotate among your companies so that we maintain efficiency."

He closed his eyes, smiling slightly, basking in his genius.

"This is the beginning of the end. The Adversary's accursed and miserable end. I alone am invincible. Imitate me, brothers, and you will *begin* to see what it means to be a god. What good will the Adversary's son do for these monkeys when I have turned him into food for wild dogs and vultures?"

+

The Master haunted the disciples' steps. He had no shadow of his own, so he would hide in theirs. They did nothing without his notice, his keen eyes catching every movement. Jesus had been held up from his journey by a woman who was healed by simply touching his tunic as he passed through a crowd. He praised her, holding her up as a model of bold faith, and returned to his original task. A sick young girl needed to be healed. Her father, the ruler of the local synagogue, came to the Aberration, begging him to lay his hands on the child to heal her. All these parasites just clambering about to get healed. How amusing.

As they arrived, the sound of weeping encircled the ruler's house. His heart began to race as the sound reached his ears. He ran toward the house, desperate to know that he was mistaken, that they were crying about something else. Old women wailed, covering their faces with bony, spotted hands, aching with fresh loss and remembering their own from years past. Men stood and sat quietly, their faces and hearts weighed down with grief. The ruler's father shook with silent sobs. Approaching the ruler slowly, his brother opened his mouth to speak, his face betraying the news before he could.

"No. No. Oh, God. Please, no, no!"

"I am so sorry, Jairus. I am so sorry. She is gone. There is no need to trouble the master further," he said, mournfully.

"Oh, God! Oh, G..."

Jairus choked on the name, tears stinging his eyes.

The Master could not resist.

Why did God let this happen? Doesn't he listen at all? Doesn't he care?

Falling to his knees, the ruler wept openly for his daughter. His only daughter. The light of his eyes. The joy of his soul. Gone.

Placing his hand on Jairus' shoulder, the Aberration spoke kindly.

61

"Do not be afraid. Only believe, and she shall be made whole."

The Master braced himself against the anxiety that tried to seize him. Can he raise the dead? Where in any of the Scriptures was that ever even hinted at? Perhaps Ezekiel. But that wasn't talking about the Messiah. Was it? Apart from that, that old book was so cryptic anyway, which he hated.

Jairus looked up at the Aberration, his green eyes full of pain.

"Come with me. Bring your wife," Jesus said. He turned to his disciples, pointing to them. "Peter, James, John, you're coming, too."

James and John did not know what to make of it. Why them? They stepped forward hesitantly. Peter came forward quickly, his face radiating absolute confidence in the Aberration's wisdom. This was not the first time that Peter responded in such a manner, the Master noticed. He was quite unlike the others in this respect. Even if Peter failed to understand why the Aberration said or did certain things, he always trusted him completely. And with this trust, he was willing to follow the Aberration into dangers unknown and unthinkable.

Tears still flowing, Jairus led the Aberration, Peter, James, and John into his house. The Master stuck closely to Peter. Stifled weeping filled the dimly lit room. The thin young girl lay still on a bed into which her mother buried her face, pulling her hair as she cried. Sensing the presence of others, she raised her head, looking to her husband with confusion. Who were these men? She stood, saying nothing, looking to Jairus for an explanation. Silently, the Aberration moved to the side of the bed, looking down on the girl compassionately. Peter, James, and John watched, unsure of what to do.

"Little girl," the Aberration said softly, "arise."

She opened her eyes as if from a deep sleep and propped herself up on her elbows, smiling at him. Her parents' mouths and eyes widened in blessed shock. They fell on her, praising God, smothering her with kisses.

The Master growled and leaped straight to the Keep.

Bowing, the Guardian attempted to greet the Master before being hammered with a question.

"Did you lose someone just now?" the Master asked sharply.

"Lose someone, my Lord?" the Guardian replied, stunned.

"You heard me, God damn it! Did you just lose someone?!" he barked.

Taken aback, the Guardian stammered, "My Lord, that is quite impossible. You know that better than anyone."

"She might have escaped your notice. It was a just a little girl. Twelve years old. Jewish. Just now," he pressed urgently. "Is it possible that she might have been taken away?"

The Guardian had never looked so confused. He shook his head incredulously.

"No, my Lord. It is *not* possible. Taken away by whom? The Adversary himself doesn't know about this place. I tell you, no one has left, and no one is going to."

Unconvinced, the Master leaped back to Jairus' house. The sounds of bedazzled joy carried even further than the cries of misery that hung in the air only moments before. Disgusted, the Master watched as the girl sat in her mother's lap, her father feeding her fish. Had she really died? Or had her breath or heartbeat simply grown too faint to notice?

Severe sickness had brought the girl close to death, and everyone thought she was dead. That was it. It had to be. How could he have been so recklessly afraid? He gave a single relieved laugh. The Aberration was a healer and a teacher, and that was all.

Jairus' brother began to pour wine for the rejoicing family and friends. Peter, James, and John sat next to the Aberration, receiving their cups with gratitude. The Master's eyes narrowed. He saw clearly that the Aberration prized Peter as a model of faith, an exemplar of trust. This was good. When a giant fell, everyone noticed.

+

Buying bread for the Aberration and the disciples was Judas' job. No one assigned it to him, he just always volunteered. In the bustling marketplace at Tyre, Judas paid the baker for the fresh loaves now in his large rough cloth bag.

Slinging it over his left shoulder, he pressed his way back into the crowd humming to himself. The hot dry air of the cloudless day smelled of eastern spices, cooking meat, and dust. Nowhere was Judas more at home than in a market. He loved the sounds of haggling, talking, and laughter. The sight of fine wares from distant and exotic places filled him with excitement.

The Master walked beside him through the press, studying his joyful face as he basked in the noises, sights, and smells of the place. They came upon a textile merchant to their right, his stand shaded by a weathered tan cloth, but holding stacks of expensive silks and linens. A tall angry customer shouted and cursed at the squat round merchant for raising the price upon which they had just agreed. Nodding at the Voice standing nearby, whispering to the tall man, the Master turned his attention back to Judas. Obscenities poured from the tall man violently on the merchant, still sitting, regarding the raging man with calm disdain. The tall man could take no more. He punched the fat merchant squarely in the jaw, knocking his money box to the ground, sending coins flying into the crowded path. Like swine on freshly thrown slop, the passersby descended on the money, furiously grabbing at all they could handle. Judas turned to watch the commotion with curiosity. Two denarii rolled straight toward his feet. As if by reflex, he put his dusty sandaled foot on the coins and scooted them through the dirt to himself. He scooped them up quickly and put them in his purse in a single motion.

How about a drink, now?

Judas licked his lips slightly and made his way to the wine vendor. Just a small wineskin to finish before returning to Jesus. He savored every mouthful of the sweet wine as he perused the merchants' goods. A long leather necklace with a small ivory pendant caught his eye.

There's a pretty thing.

Half a denarius. Done. He put it on, hiding it beneath his tunic. The wine began to make him feel lightheaded, so he followed his nose to the scent of roasting lamb.

Just a bit before heading back to the Master.

He licked the grease from his fingers and wiped them on his clothes as he chewed the last of the tender lamb. And now, back to camp. Three prostitutes sitting in the shade by the gate of an inn caught his eye as he passed on the way back.

How about it, then?

He sighed. Such a shame. Not enough time for that. Still, life was rather sweet.

The Master followed him back to camp. This little thief did not disappoint. Making his way down to the dock where the Aberration and the disciples were staying, Judas held up the bag of bread for all to see.

"Time to eat!" he called out jovially.

He handed a loaf to each man who thanked him sincerely.

"May the Lord bless you, brother," said Peter.

Judas smiled and waved his hand dismissively. "Don't mention it."

Lastly, he made his way to the Aberration sitting by the shore, looking out at the water.

"For you, Master," he said, giving Jesus a sizeable loaf.

The Aberration turned to him and smiled, receiving the bread.

"Thank you, dear Judas."

The two of them made their way to the other disciples who gathered close together. Once assembled, the Aberration gave the blessing.

"Blessed art Thou, Lord our God, King of the universe, Who bringeth forth bread from the earth."

They broke their bread and ate heartily, talking of small matters. Andrew, James, and John shared fishing stories. Thomas, Bartholomew, and Judas Thaddeus spoke of their favorite dishes back home. Simon the Zealot and Philip had little to say, commenting occasionally on the next day's journey. Matthew and his brother James talked of the weather with Jesus. Peter and Judas Iscariot discussed their joy at being chosen to accompany the Aberration on his mission.

Outside the circle, the Master eyed Peter and Judas as they went on and on about their happiness. He folded his arms pensively. Such different men, he thought. One brave and trusting, impetuous but devoted. The other vain and greedy, charming but dishonest. One simple but deeply moral. The other clever but devious. Of all the men in this circle, these two would prove most effective, the Master calculated. Judas Iscariot would be no problem. Throw a bone, and like a slobbering dog, he would run to catch it.

Peter, on the other hand, would require a little work.

+

Jehuda the Pharisee arrived at the synagogue later than usual. His servant had not drawn enough water for the daily washings the day before, and now it was the Sabbath. He was in an ill temper because he had to draw the water himself.

The venerable sights and smells of the holy place did nothing to improve his mood. Finding his way to his usual seat up front, he saw Jesus preparing to read from the Torah. He had seen him once before and had heard terrible stories about him. Eating with sinners. Not keeping the Sabbath. Some nonsense about him healing sick people, cleansing lepers, and such. And now *he* was going to read from the Law to them? He sat sighing with irritation, pulling at his gray beard.

The Master stood at the far end of the bema, filled only with Pharisees.

He does not honor the Sabbath day to keep it holy.

Murmuring among themselves, the Pharisees grumbled about the Aberration's presence.

Put him to the test. Do you see poor Elihu with his withered hand over there? Bring him to this flouter of Moses' Law, and see what he does.

Jesus rose to read the Scriptures. As he approached the scroll, Jehuda stood and spoke.

"Good Rabbi, I have a question for you."

Quickly, he crossed the synagogue floor to get Elihu. Pulling him by the arm, he brought him before the Aberration. Elihu and the congregation in general seemed confused.

"Is it lawful to heal on the Sabbath?" he asked, studying the Aberration's expression. Jehuda lifted up Elihu's gnarled right hand, which was little more than bones covered with shriveled gray skin. The Pharisee did not expect to witness anything miraculous; he only hoped to confirm what he had heard about the Aberration or perhaps to trap him in his words.

Placing his hands on the scroll, the Aberration addressed him and the whole congregation who looked on.

"Which of you men that has a sheep which falls into a pit on the Sabbath day will not take hold of it and lift it out?"

He stared intently at Jehuda.

"How much better is a man than a sheep?"

Jehuda remained indignantly silent. No one answered. Each Pharisee seated on the bema shot venomous glances at the Aberration with his contaminated hands on the holy Scriptures.

Jesus opened the scroll.

"It is lawful to do good on the Sabbath."

Does he instruct you who know and revere the Law of Moses?

"Stretch out your hand," he said, facing Elihu.

The confused man put out his skeletal hand, Jehuda still holding his arm. Flesh filled the spaces between bones, covering and binding them. A meaty palm formed and fingers rounded out, taking on a healthy color. He raised his left hand in amazement, comparing it with his right. Identical. Jehuda gasped, releasing his arm and stepping backward. Elihu flexed the fingers of his restored right hand and looked up at Jesus, speechless.

He profanes the Sabbath day in the presence of all those here. With his hands on the Books of the Law. Has he no shame? You have seen it with your own eyes.

All at once, the Pharisees filed out of the synagogue, the stamping of their feet and the rustling of their garments echoing until, at last, none of them remained. The Master followed them outside.

The audacity. The gall of this upstart.

The Pharisees cursed and spat.

The prince of devils has given him this power. He is in league with Satan.

Jehuda hailed the attention of the others.

"Brethren, we have a problem that needs to be fixed."

+

Screaming, the Tormentor left the blind and mute young man face down on the rocky ground.

He opened his eyes, raising his head, seeing the astounded faces surrounding him. Awe washed over him. The Aberration extended his hand to him. Ecstatic at the brightness, shapes, colors, and lines around him, he took his hand, standing slowly.

"Praise be to God," he uttered, surprised by the sound of his own voice.

A young woman covered her mouth with her hands, tears filling her eyes. She ran to his side. The demon had taken his sight and speech from him years ago, and now the demon was gone. She embraced her husband, wetting his face with tears of thanksgiving. The witnesses nearby gave thanks to God.

"This is the Son of David, is it not?" asked a lean, elderly man.

Your Messiah.

The crowd buzzed with the question and affirmations.

"He will open the eyes of the blind," added a beardless youth, his voice brimming with excitement.

He will open the eyes of the blind. He will restore the kingdom.

Louder and louder, the people spoke, bound together in euphoria, exulting in the joy of their impending deliverance.

The Romans will crumble beneath his feet. Their blood shall run in the streets. He shall drive them out with his sword and sit upon David's throne for a thousand years. Your Messiah. All hail!

Their hearts ached sweetly with hope and adoration as they beheld their Messiah. Here in the dust and the heat of the day. The King of Israel. At last.

A party of Pharisees scolded the wide-eyed people for their slavish stupidity, their gross ignorance of the Law and the customs of their fathers.

"He casts out devils by the prince of devils!" shouted a young Pharisee with a trimmed brown beard. He shook his authoritative finger in the Aberration's face.

His power comes from Satan. These mindless sheep follow the devil's agent.

Other Pharisees raised their angry voices, affirming the truth of this just charge.

The beardless youth stepped forward, challenging the Pharisees.

"Has it ever been seen since the beginning of the world that a man has opened the eyes of the blind?"

Praises and curses, chants and jeers swept over the crowd like opposing winds, whirling into a storm of hatred and devotion.

Messiah.

Prince of devils.

The King of Israel, defeater of the Romans.

Liar. Blasphemer.

The Aberration spoke, silencing the argument.

"Every kingdom divided against itself is brought to desolation, and every city or house divided against itself shall not stand. If Satan casts out Satan, then he is divided against himself. Then, how will his kingdom stand?"

Take that, you damned Pharisees. This is the King of Israel, and his kingdom will never be divided.

Staring with odium, the Pharisees could not speak.

God damn him. He rejects the Law and all that is holy. He will tear our nation apart. See how the people follow and are bewitched by this sorcerer.

He continued to speak. Almost no one listened, except for his disciples. It was enough for the people that he could perform miracles and would deliver them from their oppressors once and for all. Rome and Herod would pay in blood for the rape of Israel. Never again would there be another Egypt. Another Babylon. Another Rome. The Kingdom of Israel would sit in supreme dominion over the entire world. Near and far, the peoples of the earth would bow toward Jerusalem forever. Seated on his throne in a glorious new palace, the Son of David would exact justice for his people. The chosen people. And they were blessed to see him and be near him before his reign would begin.

+++

Lucifer loved his position. Serving the Lord by directing the other orders of angels brought him a deep sense of satisfaction. As he worked alongside the other Archangels, it became increasingly clear to him that he was the most capable of all of them. His fellows admired his charisma and his natural ability as a leader. Everyone loved him, especially the Lord. Initially, Lucifer accepted this as a fact of life — he was gifted, and he was loved because of it. His peers and the Lord recognized him as the most glorious of the Archangels. And that is what bothered him.

The Lord, as far as Lucifer could tell, did not love him any more than the others. If he did, he certainly made no outward show of it. Why not? Was Lucifer not the most glorious of all the Archangels? As the thought grew within him, he noticed an unsettling change in his surroundings. The light which illuminated all things started to seem harsh. Still revealing, but no longer gentle. Bright, but no longer comforting. He was curious if anyone else noticed.

"Michael," he said, almost whispering.

"Yes, brother?" Michael gave Lucifer his full attention.

"Have you perceived any alteration in the light? Does it seem changed in any manner to you?" he asked, studying the light.

"How would it change?" asked Michael, clearly not understanding.

"Does it seem to you that it lacks the gentleness it once had?"

Michael stared at him, puzzled. "That's absurd," he began. "It is as brilliant and as invigorating as it has always been."

Without a word, Lucifer turned away.

+++

Had the Master been mortal, his tireless pursuit of the Aberration would have exhausted him to death. He raised his chin confidently, admiring his own boundless strength, his limitless intellect. The Aberration had sent the twelve out by two's into cities and towns which he would visit later. He gave his friends the ability to perform miracles like him, instructing them to prepare the people of these places for his visit. He sent out another seventy to do the same thing. Some places were interested, and others were not. It always got ugly when the disciples cast Tormentors out of their victims. The Master would berate them furiously for not standing their ground.

Amid the tension of guiding the Council to sway the people, the disciples, and the religious authorities, the Master received word that John the Baptist had been killed exactly as he had asked. Cold comfort, he thought. The Baptist was only a thorn that needed to be plucked out. The Aberration was a spear as thick as a weaver's beam. After John's death, the Aberration had fed over five thousand of his own people with five small loaves of bread and two fish. He did the same for over four thousand Gentiles with seven loaves. In spite of the wonders, the Master's plan seemed to be working. The Pharisees, Sadducees, scribes, and priests hated the Aberration and wanted him dead, though they never made any formal plans. The people and his disciples loved him, the Great Liberator of Israel.

Peter had been the Master's particular focus, lately. At times, it seemed that Peter accepted everything the Master whispered to him. At others, it seemed as though he heard nothing at all. It was difficult for him to calculate exactly how Peter would crack, since there were times in which he seemed impervious to the Master's influence. Every night before Peter slept, he prayed to the Adversary that the Kingdom of Israel would soon be restored. The Master encouraged him as he prayed.

At Caesarea Philippi, the Aberration and the disciples made their camp near a patch of cedars and hearty shrubs. They had finished the evening meal and sat talking beneath the tall cedars, the western sky turning orange, dyeing the clouds dark blue. The Master took his usual place outside the circle.

Putting aside familiar topics, the Aberration asked the disciples a question.

"Who do people say I am?"

They were somewhat amused as they repeated the rumors of the people.

"Some say you are John the Baptist returned from the dead," piped up Bartholomew.

"Some say Elijah or Jeremiah or one of the other prophets," added Simon the Zealot.

They all laughed good-naturedly.

"Who do *you* say I am?" asked the Aberration.

Silence replaced the laughter. They looked at one another with apprehension, unthreatened but unsure. Inwardly, each man had asked himself this question but could never quite articulate an answer. Who was he, really? They were pretty sure, but they could not say they knew. So they were silent. All except Peter.

He spoke with unswerving certainty.

"I say you are the Messiah, the Son of the living God."

The Master was not surprised by Peter's boldness. He folded his arms.

Turning to Peter, the Aberration placed his hand on his shoulder.

"Blessed are you Simon, son of Jonah, for flesh and blood have not revealed this to you, but my Father who is in Heaven. And I also say to you that you are Peter, and upon this rock will I build my Church. And the gates of hell shall not prevail against it. And I will give to you the keys of the Kingdom of Heaven. And whatsoever you shall bind on earth shall be bound in Heaven, and whatsoever you loose on earth shall be loosed in Heaven."

"That's rich," whispered the Master inaudibly. "Animals having an effect on the throne room of the Adversary."

The Aberration's demeanor became grave.

"Tell no one what you know. It is not yet time. The Son of Man must suffer many things and be rejected by the elders and the chief priests and the scribes. And be killed. And be raised on the third day."

Taken aback, the Master's arms fell to his side. Did the Aberration know the plan? How could he possibly know about his impending death? Was the Adversary sending him messages? He was certainly going to fall catastrophically short of the people's expectations of him, so perhaps he had some inkling that his mission would end abruptly. Even so, did he honestly think that his pathetic group of devotees could possibly continue the work he was doing? They were all so weak, and the Master would certainly humiliate and destroy them all with the greatest ease.

Shocked and partially offended, Peter halfway shouted, "What?"

His face alight with determination and devotion, he stepped up quickly to the Aberration, taking him by the shoulders.

"No, Lord! This shall *never* happen to you!"

The Aberration spoke sternly and quickly, looking Peter in the eyes.

"Get behind me, Satan! You are an offense to me, for you do not think on the things of God, but those of men."

Startled, Peter backed away, nearly tripping. The words stung him, and yet he felt no bitterness.

Vexing confusion nearly choked the Master. He was utterly at a loss. He had not whispered anything like this to Peter. It was true that he desperately wanted the disciples and the people to burn with religious fervor and be willing to shed blood in the Aberration's name, but why would the Aberration say something like that? Was he speaking to Peter or to him? Did he know that the Master was there, hiding from human sight? Was it a message to back down? Not a minute ago, the

Aberration had called Peter "blessed," and now he seemed to call him "Satan."

Satan. The Master had always hated that name. It was not even a name; it just meant "adversary." And, of course, there was only one Adversary. And there was only one Master.

He leaped to a desolate field, disregarding his surroundings. It was time to think without distraction. Never before had he dealt with such a challenge. His confidence in himself did not waver. He was more than equal to the task. But for the first time, he began to feel the burden of time. He was mired in it. Until the Aberration was dead, the Master would be chained to the coming moments, days, weeks, months. If the plan was to work, he could not cut corners simply to speed events along. He had to be patient. But the patience was excruciating. The Aberration had bent logic and certainty beyond recognition, and for that he had to die. Only when the Aberration was dead and rotting in his grave could the Master return to the pleasure and peace of his kingdom.

+

Day and night, people flocked to the Aberration's camp on the Jordan River seeking healing. It was in the same spot that John the Baptist began his mission, so it was well known. From some, he asked for a show of faith. From others, he asked for nothing at all. To all, he granted their requests. That was until a messenger arrived early one morning, asking him to please come quickly. A young man, dusty with travel bowed deeply before him, breathing heavily from running.

"Lord, your dear friend Lazarus is sick," he managed between breaths.

The disciples knew Lazarus and his sisters, Mary and Martha, and they knew that they were close to Jesus. Immediately, they began folding up their camp.

"This sickness is not unto death," said the Aberration, "but for the glory of God, that the Son of God might be glorified by it."

Taking his response as an assent to go see Lazarus, the young man rose and headed back in the direction from which he came. The Aberration turned to the disciples packing up their things.

"There is no need for that. We are not leaving now," he said.

They were all puzzled.

"Lord, Bethany is two days from here. If you want to heal Lazarus, we need to leave now. The news from that young man is already two days old," Philip said, his youthful face creased with concern.

Smiling, the Aberration placed his hand on Philip's shoulder.

How odd, the Master thought. He always jumped at these kinds of opportunities, and now he was staying put? The Master continued to watch closely, almost mechanically.

Two days passed on the bank of the Jordan River. People wanting to be healed, to see, or to walk

came and went as they had before. They rejoiced and
went on their different ways. Moloch and Chemosh
kept hard at work whispering to them as they came
and went. Some of the disciples were mildly
disturbed that the Aberration seemed to ignore his
friend who needed healing. Perhaps Lazarus was not
as ill as the young man made out. After all, Jesus did
say that Lazarus' sickness was "not unto death."
Maybe it was not that bad. On the morning of the
third day, he spoke to the disciples.

"Let us go into Judea again."

"Master," Andrew began, "they wanted to
stone you the last time we were there, and you want
to go back?"

"Aren't there twelve hours in the day? If any
man walks in the day, he does not stumble because
he sees the light of this world. But if a man walks in
the night, he stumbles because there is no light in
him."

Blank stares met his words. They did not
understand. But they did understand enough to
know that he knew what he was talking about.
Packing their gear, they followed him as he walked
toward Bethany.

Nervous anticipation filled the silence as the
disciples made their way down the road behind the
Aberration. What kind of near misses and scrapes
would they get into this time? Last winter when they
were in Jerusalem, he told the Pharisees that he was
one with the Father. From the shadows, the Master
stirred them up to the height of righteous

indignation. They tried to stone him, but he got away. The Master felt that the time was not quite right.

A day into their journey, still no one spoke. The Master followed soundlessly as ever. Low clouds blanketed the sky, holding the sweltering heat close to the ground. Each traveler wore a layer of sweat mixed with dust; as new drops of sweat emerged, they too coagulated with the dust. The dryness of their throats only served to sharpen the anxiety pricking them as they walked toward only God knew what. They made their camp at the foot of a rocky hill two hundred or so yards to the right of the road. The only words spoken were the blessing of the bread before they retired for the evening. A fitful sleep jostled half of them, while the other half could not sleep at all. Thunder gave a muffled boom from the south. Watching the uneasy men sleep, the Master made rounds, whispering into their dreams.

At daybreak, the Aberration rose first, uttering silent prayers. Some of the disciples offered up quick prayers as they awoke. Others simply packed their things, still shaky from the previous night's disturbed slumber. As the Aberration packed the last of his gear, he broke the silence.

"Our friend Lazarus sleeps, but I go that I may awake him out of sleep." He stood, heading for the road.

Judas Thaddeus offered his opinion.

"Lord, he will do well if he sleeps."

James nodded in agreement.

Turning back to face them, the Aberration broke the news flatly.

"Lazarus is dead."

They stopped in their tracks. All but Peter, James, and John wore expressions of complete disbelief. What were they doing, then, going into Judea where the Aberration's enemies were itching for an excuse to stone him to death? For what purpose?

"And I am glad for your sakes that I was not there, for the purpose that you might believe. Even so, let us go to him."

Fear pierced the Master again. The same fear that cut him at Jairus' house. This could not be what it seemed.

Thomas inwardly swelled with courage, emboldened by the Aberration's words. He turned to the others.

"Let us also go that we may die with him."

The others followed. But they still did not speak. The Master stung with trepidation.

Clouds broke, letting the hot sun bear down on them before they arrived in Bethany. More sweat and dust. The whole company was sore with walking and needed to rest. Lazarus' house stood on the west side of the road and a mile from the city. As the Aberration and the disciples approached it, they were greeted with more silence. The house doors were open. Dozens of men and women sat in sackcloth outside the house. Some sat at the door of the tomb eighty yards to the rear of the house.

Weeping. The young man who carried word of Lazarus' illness saw the Aberration drawing closer and went into the house to inform Mary and Martha that he had arrived.

Sobbing, clutching her black veil tightly around her chin, Martha ran out and stopped before the Aberration.

"Lord," she cried, "if you had been here, my brother would not have died." She fell to her knees, shaking. "But I know that even now, whatever you ask of God, he will give to you."

Her grief made him sad.

"Your brother shall rise again," he said firmly.

She looked up at him, her hazel eyes streaming tears.

"I know he shall rise again in the resurrection at the last day," she moaned, sobbing again.

His brown eyes narrowed.

"I am the resurrection and the life. He who believes in me, even if he dies, shall live. And whoever lives and believes in me shall never die." He paused. "Do you believe this?"

She wiped away her tears and stood.

"Yes, Lord. I believe that you are the Messiah, the Son of God, who has come into the world."

The former irrational fear hammered at the Master's mind as he watched Martha run back to her house. No, he thought. Stop it. There is nothing to be concerned about. You know well of the Aberration's love for allegory and metaphor. He is waxing poetic, as usual.

Mary ran out, crying feverishly, falling at the Aberration's feet, dust whipping around her.

His throat tightened as sorrow twisted his face. He wept with her. For several moments, he stood crying in the hot sun, tears cutting rivers down his dirty face.

Curiosity dampened the Master's anxiety. He had never seen Jesus cry before. How marvelous.

Still weeping, the Aberration asked where Lazarus was buried. The group of mourners led him toward the tomb, a cave covered by a heavy stone. Mary and Martha walked slowly beside him, Mary still sobbing. Slowly, they gathered at the tomb. The dull ache of mourning pressed down on them. As Mary, Martha, and the others cried, some looked to the Aberration. The ache grew sharper as it mingled with bitter disappointment. Lazarus was gone. Jesus could have stopped it. But he was not here. He was not here. The Aberration stared at the rounded stone covering the cave. Silently. Wiping his face on his sleeve, his sadness was diminished by something new. Anger. His eyes grew fierce as he stared at the dead white stone.

"Take away the stone," he said, flatly.

The Master leaped to his side frantically. No, this could not be. It was impossible. He couldn't do this.

Martha pleaded, "Lord, by this time there will be a stench. He has been dead for *four* days."

He spoke softly but firmly.

"Didn't I say to you that if you would believe, you should see the glory of God?"

Looking to the four men standing by the stone, the Aberration nodded his head commandingly. They strained and grunted, heaving the massive stone away. As the mouth of the cave opened, the putrid stench of decay belched out upon them. Two of them covered their noses and mouths with their sleeves. Two of them retched violently on the dusty ground, grabbing their stomachs. The Master raced into the tomb, touching the body. Absolutely dead, wrapped up in bands just as the Jews had learned in Egypt. Beneath the taut gauzy bands congealed with aloes and myrrh, the Master could see that the corpse was fully bloated from the heat. He stared in a panic at the Aberration standing several feet from the mouth of the tomb. The Aberration was praying, his arms raised.

"Lazarus! Come forth!" he shouted.

The dead man sat up rapidly as if waking from a nightmare. Horror coursed through the Master and froze him as he watched the man breathe deeply and stand on his feet, taking ridiculously small steps toward the daylight on account of his bound feet. The bloating was gone, and the soggy grave bands sagged as he walked forward.

Moloch and Chemosh stood petrified. The Master leaped to the Keep, his silver eyes livid and wild.

"God damn! No! No! No!"

+

"What happened, Ashteroth?!" shouted the Master, seizing the Guardian by his tunic at the neck.

The Guardian, reeled with the double shock of what he had just witnessed and the Master's fury. His head craned around to a spot behind him.

"It happened over there," he said, shakily, pointing to the spot. "In all the ages I have been down here, I have never seen anything like it."

The Master, who had only ever known the Guardian to wear a countenance of stone-like vigilance and voyeuristic fascination, was disturbed to see him wear an expression of genuine terror. He released his grip, following the Guardian's finger.

"It was over there," he repeated.

Far into the blackness, a sizeable group of prisoners formed an uneven circle, facing inwardly. Some of their faces reflected the same fear possessing the Master and the Guardian. Some reflected inspired hope. Others, startled curiosity. One elderly man raised his hands in prayer, praising God for his kindness.

"I distinctly remember that there was one next to that old man. He...he had not been here long. A young man just beyond forty years old. And then..." The Guardian's golden eyes widened. "...it was like...a pinprick...a pinprick of light...and then he was gone..." he trailed off.

Unable to believe, the Master squinted at the thought.

"Light?" he whispered. His eyes scanned the abyss above them.

The Guardian turned to him and nodded.

"Quicker than the blink of an eye. I have never seen anything like it down here."

Mouths open and faces bent with consternation, the Master and the Guardian stood speechlessly. This was not possible. The Adversary did not even know the Keep existed, or if he did, he certainly never showed any interest in it. Closing his mouth, the Master set his teeth and fixed his gaze on the prisoners. This was his kingdom. Everything that he ever worked for. His one haven in the otherwise hideously grotesque universe fashioned by the Adversary. The Master's eye twitched. It seemed that the ether had taken on some strange quality that it did not have before. A sound.

The Master honed in on the sound and leaped in its general direction. He stopped just short of its source at the base of a slight upward incline in the ground. He recognized this one. His eyes projected the venom seething within him. John the Baptist.

He spoke in death to the captives locked in darkness with the same passion he had in life. His eyes closed, he projected his voice to the crowd surrounding him.

"The Son of God is coming to you! Make your hearts ready! He comes to you soon! Your deliverance is at hand!"

Now, the mystery was revealed. Perfectly.

All of the Master's doubts and fears vanished. The Adversary's scheme lay plainly before his silver eyes, glistening with certainty. He planned to steal the Master's prisoners one by one. How infinitely despicable, even for the Adversary. Truly, he had sunk to a new low. First, it was the refusal to give the Master his due. Then, it was the talking apes. And now, this. Icy hatred and adamantine resolution fused within his swelling chest, creating an indestructible alloy that not even the Adversary with all his strength could break. The Master needed to kill the Aberration soon. Otherwise, there was no telling how many prisoners he might lose. Even to the last one.

It would not be enough to stone him to death. He needed to be crushed and humiliated mercilessly before the eyes of the whole world. In the process, the religious authorities would be hollowed out with their bitter envy. The people would be corrupted by their tribal fervor and bloodlust. And the disciples, they would be utterly ruined by their cowardice and despair. There was not a moment to lose. For the first time ever, time was not on the Master's side.

+

In the council room of the Royal Stoa, the Pharisees' and priests' faces hung heavy with dire concern. News of Lazarus spread like fire over dry grass throughout Jerusalem and the surrounding cities. It reached all of the Pharisees, Saducees, scribes, and priests the same day Lazarus emerged from his tomb. They pulled at their beards, shifted in their seats, fidgeted with their garments, and rocked nervously as their frenetic discussion echoed to the high ceiling above them. Caiaphas, the high priest, sat silently on his ornate throne, his pales eyes and prematurely wrinkled face aglow with disdain and anger. The Master, his heart coiled like an asp ready to strike, stood beside him, a single pale hand on the armrest of the throne. His concentration on the dynamics of the room was so sharp that he paid no attention to the Elder and Asmodeus standing at opposite ends of the gathering.

Jehuda raised his voice above the din, gesticulating violently.

"Are any of you listening? What are we going to do? He performs miracles! If we let him alone, then all of Judea will believe in him, and the Romans will come and take *everything* we have. Pilate already has a taste for our blood. Imagine that combined with Caesar's full military support. There will be nothing left!"

Fevered voices of assent and suggested plans hurtled across the room, landing nowhere. Caiaphas put his hand to his aching temple, closing his eyes in frustration.

Ultimately, Pilate is the problem. He will butcher you when he gets wind of a potential revolution. That is unless, you make him the solution.

His eyes opened, and he shouted with conviction.

"Imbeciles! You know nothing!" The bile in his voice silenced them as it rang in their ears. "Have you not considered that it might be necessary for one man to die so that an entire nation avoids destruction?!"

Take him to Pilate.

The council did not need an explanation; they understood. The Master grimaced. That was quicker than my Council, he thought.

In a calmer tone, Caiaphas asked, "Does anyone know where he is now?"

Jehuda stood.

"I have it on good authority that he is in Ephraim at the moment."

Stepping down from his throne, Caiaphas looked at the floor, his hands folded behind his back. A grizzled old Pharisee, his eyes clouded thickly with cataracts, put a question before the council with his frail, raspy voice.

"Does anyone think he will come to Jerusalem for the Passover?"

Caiaphas paced toward him.

"If he does, we must be ready and waiting. Keep your eyes and ears open. We cannot lay a finger on him out among the people unless we want a full scale riot. We must do it quietly. When we do," he paused, "our case against him must be flawless. Take heed that you recall his every offense against the Law." He turned, walking slowly back to his throne. "We will meet again tomorrow. In the meantime, brethren, *watch.*"

Kill this Lazarus, too. It is because of him that the people run to this Jesus.

"Chief priests, stay behind for a moment," he added.

Pharisees and scribes rose from their seats, rapt in earnest conversation as they left the great hall. The Master signaled to the Elder and Asmodeus to follow them. Caiaphas waited until the last of them filed out and the heavy cedar doors closed. He sat.

"Brethren, it does not seem right that we should leave behind any trace of this deceiver's work."

+

Martha made sure everyone's cup was full of wine. The brightly lit room hummed sweetly with joyful conversation and laughter. Pure mirth exuded from the warm light of the open windows into the deepening blue of the evening. At the table, the Aberration took a sip of wine and quickly set his cup down as he passed a large bowl of hot lentils to Lazarus, who was already on his fourth helping. "Thank you, Lord," he said with his mouth full as the Aberration spooned out more into his bowl. The whole house was filled with Lazarus' family, neighbors, and friends. An occasional spectator would approach the house, looking in for just a glimpse of the man who was raised from the dead. There he was, eating heartily at the table next to Jesus, the promised Messiah.

The Passover drew closer, and with it, the trip to Jerusalem. But there was far too much to celebrate now to think of it. Lazarus was alive, and that was all that mattered to his family and his friends. Mary stood up from her place near the Aberration and crossed the room to a tall shelf laden with cooking supplies. Reaching up as far as her arms could stretch, she retrieved a small jar, cradling it carefully as she returned to the table. She kneeled at the Aberration's feet, not looking up, and opened it. Taking his bare feet, she poured the entire jar of ointment on them. The overwhelmingly rich fragrance of spikenard wafted through the house, even to the windows and door. Judas Iscariot sat erect as he recognized the scent. He grimaced as he watched Mary spread the ointment thoroughly over the Aberration's feet. She removed the veil from her head, letting down her long curly black hair to wipe his feet, her hands and hair taking on the sweet fragrance. The Aberration smiled gently at her.

Judas could not resist.

"Why wasn't this ointment sold for three hundred denarii and given to the poor?"

Raising his eyes to Judas, the Aberration said, "Leave her alone. She has kept this for the day of my burial. You will always have the poor with you, but you will not always have me."

Judas looked down and tried to conceal his humiliation. He left the table. What was that all about? Everyone in the house heard his words. Was it necessary to call him out like that? The sting gave

93

way to anger, and he stepped outside the house, forgetting his shoes. In the darkness outside, Judas fumed alone, refusing to look back at the warmth inside. He spit on the ground as anger became rage. Poised at Judas' back, the Master placed his pale hand on his shoulder.

Who the hell does he think he is, really?

Judas turned around, surprised. He thought he heard something.

Grinning icily, the Master sank his hands into Judas' heart and disappeared into him. Judas' eyes clenched painfully shut as he doubled over. The Master pulled him straight like a taut rope. Judas opened his eyes to the darkness surrounding him with the inspired enthusiasm of revelation. He needed to go to Jerusalem. Now. He headed toward the road in his bare feet. It was time. Time to be rid of Jesus of Nazareth. At times it had been fun, but now Jesus had crossed the line, and now he would pay. Pay…Maybe his enemies could pay, too. Pay Judas. Excellent idea. Perhaps the best idea he ever had. Kept it for the day of his burial? You're damn right she has. Jerusalem was a little more than two miles away. Not far.

As Judas made it to the road, a river of curses poured from his mouth. His life was an endless list of grievances that needed to be hammered, crushed, and obliterated with his tongue. His parents. Home town. Enemies. Friends. Sicknesses. Women. Failures. Disappointments. Work. Sadness. Aches. Inconveniences. Rabbis. Wasted time. God. Jesus.

God damn it all. He cursed rabidly and drooled as he struck out further through the darkness.

Distance and time meant nothing. Sharp rocks and cuts on his feet hurt but did not stop him from plodding forward. Where? Where was he? The gate. Jerusalem. Very good. He needed to go to the council room of the chief priests at the Temple. He didn't even know where it was. Details, details. Wasn't it late? When he got there, would they even be there? They would be there. They would be having a meeting. Yes, yes. He must trust his instincts. They would lead him every time. Every time.

He found himself before an enormous double door. Lebanon cedar. Nice. This was it. He let himself in. Caiaphas, the chief priests, and several of the Pharisees stared at him, incensed at his brazen interruption of their meeting. Jehuda and some of the others recognized him and approached him, ready to tear him with their own hands.

"What is the meaning of this? How dare you..."

"How can I help, reverend elders?" Judas cut him off.

+++

This was personal.

The Lord had purposefully targeted Lucifer, slighted him under the guise of love. But why? Had he not done everything the Lord asked him? Had he not carried out his

95

labors with supreme precision and excellence? The answer came almost as quickly as the question.

Envy.

Lucifer was the most magnificent of all the Lord's creations. Too magnificent. In creating Lucifer, it was altogether possible that the Lord had put something into him, which he could not get back. Something lost to him for all eternity.

That was it.

When he created Lucifer, the Lord had given away the most precious part of himself — that which made him Lord in the first place. It was all so clear. As Lucifer's realization grew, so did the intensity of the light. It was too bright. And hot. No doubt, the Lord was onto him.

As he performed his duties directing the angels to their tasks, he took each of them aside, saying the same thing each time: "I thank you for your labors, and I appreciate all you do. Has the Lord ever thanked you?" Most angels never answered or replied, "It matters not."

Soon, however, a prominent Power answered with great irritation, "No. He never has."

Lucifer replied, "We will talk more about this later. I am interested in what you have to say, Ba'al."

+++

Word got out that the Aberration would come into Jerusalem early in the day. Crowds of people camped out beside the road from Bethany to Jerusalem, waiting. At sunrise, those who actually slept awoke quickly, getting up to stare down the road. Travelers on the road gave curious looks at the masses awkwardly watching them pass. The cool morning air held the people's eager expectations closely around them, vibrating with delight. Today was the day. The dawn of Israel's liberation.

A small group of elderly men stood, talking of the future after the Romans were gone.

"The coronation will probably be at the Temple, don't you think?"

"I would think it would be at the palace."

"No, he will need a new palace. It isn't fitting that the rightful King of Israel, the Son of David, should live in Herod's den of iniquity."

"Oh, absolutely, but for the coronation?"

Another group of dour-faced young men speculated on the next few days.

"Does he have contacts among the Zealots?"

"One of his closest disciples is a Zealot."

"Whose forces will he use? It will be one thing to put down Herod. But Rome?"

"The Temple guards might be his force."

"It might be the case that *we* have to be his force."

At the bend in the road in the distance, the Aberration rode on a donkey. The disciples followed close behind, leading a colt carrying their gear. "It's him!" a voice shouted. The call multiplied as he drew closer. Shouts and cheers grew to a deafening roar as the people spilled into the road. A number of people cut down palm branches and waved them excitedly. He approached the edge of the crowd, and almost in automatic formation, people laid the branches and their cloaks across the road for the King of Israel.

"Hosanna! Hosanna! Blessed is he that comes in the name of the Lord!" they chanted.

Judas Iscariot's face smirked as the Master heard the other Voices.

Behold, the Vanquisher of Rome! Behold, the Scourge of Herod!

"Hosanna in the highest!"

He shall not sheath his sword until the last Roman lies dead!

"Blessed is he that comes in the name of the Lord!"

With a rod of iron he will smash them to pieces!

"Hosanna!"

Kill the filthy bastards!

The Master savored the people's enthused adulation. These flea-bitten apes cheered as he imagined they would cheer. They bowed as he planned for them to bow. They hoped as he led them to hope. Moving. Swaying. His hand had set them in motion. Cheers followed and continued to rain down on the Aberration as he entered the city. People elbowed, clawed, and climbed to behold the Messiah riding to them in humility. How many generations of their fathers had passed, hoping and praying for this moment? And there he was, before their very eyes. The King of Israel.

Where will he go first? To the palace? To Pilate?

Within the city the crowds continued to lay their garments on the road for the Aberration's passage. Every eye fixed on him, eager to know where he was going, what he would do first. Families came out of their homes, some climbing to their roofs to see him. A little boy of four pulled at his mother's sleeve, looking up at her.

"Who is that, Mama?"

"That is Jesus, the prophet from Nazareth."

"What is he doing here?"

"He is going to deliver us."

"From what?"

She smiled, patting his head.

The disciples appeared both anxious and excited as the multitudes hailed the Aberration. After all, they were chosen to help him restore the kingdom. It was exhilarating but frightening. Halfway into the city, it became clear that he was neither going into the upper city nor to Herod's palace. The masses clung to him as he headed to the eastern quarter toward the Temple. There he stopped. Alighting from his donkey, he went to the colt carrying the supplies. Reaching his hand into a rough cloth bag, he produced a bundle of cords tied together at one end. He gripped the bundle's tied end tightly in his right hand and walked toward the money changers and animal vendors in front of the Temple walls, his face hardened by singularity of purpose. The animal vendors continued to hand over lambs and turtledoves to their customers. The money changers, with varying degrees of accuracy, exchanged their customers' denarii for shekels. Without a word, he approached a money changer's table from the side. The line of waiting customers and the well-dressed money changer looked at him with irritation.

"You wait in line like everybody else, pal," shouted the money changer.

The Aberration grabbed the corner of the table, knocking it on its side. Money boxes crashed on the pavement, sending coins shooting in all directions. The customers scattered, shocked. Rearing his fist to punch the Aberration, the money changer flinched and scurried backward as the cords whipped inches from his face. He stumbled backward, knocking over the money changer next to him as the whip kept cracking. Down crashed the next table. And the next. The Aberration rushed to the animal vendors who fled, tripping over the animals and themselves. He kicked the pen walls down and whipped at the sheep's hindquarters, driving them into the crowd. A mixture of astonishment, anger, and enthusiasm stirred among the onlookers as the Aberration tore through upturning tables and smashing money boxes. To some, he seemed to demonstrate his contempt for the Holy Temple and the Law of Moses. To some, he seemed to give a foretaste of the glorious upheaval soon to come. Turtledoves flew from their opened cages as the Aberration unlatched them, even to the last one. Facing the crowd, he cast the whip on the ground.

"It is written," he shouted, "'*My house shall be called the house of prayer,*' but you have made it into a den of thieves!"

Admiration, confusion, and ire filled the air. No one spoke.

As he has purged the Temple of merchants, so shall he purge the land of Romans.

Jehuda came running from inside the Temple to see what had stopped the influx of worshippers bringing in sacrificial animals. Fury crippled his mind as he beheld the overturned tables, denarii and shekels littering the ground, lambs wandering among the gathered crowd, and the accursed rabbi from Nazareth standing with his back to it all.

So shall he lay waste to the land if you do not destroy him.

+

"That was it?" he asked incredulously.

"That was it."

The laborers circled a small fire in the lower city, warming their hands as the stars came out over Jerusalem. Most of them had seen the day's events unfold, but one of them, a blacksmith, could not get away from his work. He seemed underwhelmed that the Messiah's entry into city had not been more eventful. More dramatic. He rubbed his calloused hands more roughly over the fire.

"It doesn't make sense," he mused. "I thought he would at least recruit his forces today, if not begin the strike on Herod's palace."

"Personally, I think it was a sign representing what he is going to do to our enemies. Obviously, prayer is important to him, so he kicked the traders out of the Temple. To purify it. Next, he will purify the land," remarked a round leatherworker. "And then," he paused, inhaling, "he will exalt the land above all the earth."

Several of them nodded.

"Mark my words," he continued, "tomorrow he will start gathering forces." His black eyes glowed with hope. "I, for one, will gladly join him. It will be a blessing to see Herod and Pilate choke on their own blood for what they have done to our people."

Tomorrow. Tomorrow.

A muscular stoneworker massaged his swollen fingers, his eyes unblinking and his lips pressed in bitterness.

"Pilate killed my younger brother in Galilee. Not a day goes by that my poor mother doesn't weep her eyes red." His throat grew tight. He sniffed and wiped his nose. "And not a day goes by that I don't want to bring her that son of a bitch's head on a platter."

A gardener spat in the fire and spoke.

"He had all of my brothers crucified. Every night they come to me in my dreams and beg for revenge." His eyes were glassy with pain and hate.

The leatherworker nodded sympathetically.

"Jesus will give us vengeance, brothers. All of us."

You will see. Tomorrow he will muster his forces. He will strengthen his arm and poise his sword to strike. He will call upon you to fight. And when he does, you must fight without mercy.

Outside the southern wall of the Temple, near the Royal Stoa, servants of the scribes, elders, and chief priests also warmed themselves around a fire.

"He healed some cripples and a few blind people, I think, and then he was gone," said a young woman who was a doorkeeper for Caiaphas' father-in-law.

"No," corrected one of the elder's personal servants, "before he left, little children were praising him, calling him the Son of David. My master called him out on it, and he said something about God perfecting praise, or something." He smiled, somewhat smugly. "Really, I don't understand what my master has against him. He *is* the Son of David, and he will defeat our enemies, as far as I'm concerned."

The young woman frowned.

"But if he is supposed to fight for us, then why does he come to the Temple and cause a commotion and then go home?"

Why indeed? Is he not your liberator? Perhaps he shall act tomorrow.

"He really is strange, you have to admit," quipped a scribe's servant, squatting close to the fire. "But he's the best chance we have of getting our country back."

They huddled closer to the fire, hoping tomorrow would come quickly.

+

Early in the morning, the Aberration returned to the Temple. Confusion pervaded among those who hoped most eagerly for Israel's deliverance. What was he doing back at the Temple? The people speculated that perhaps he would first enlist the Temple guards. But soon he would need a larger force, and he would have to go elsewhere. Jerusalem swam in best guesses and rumors. Radicals and moderates alike wrung their hands and scratched their heads impatiently.

Surely he will recruit today. Surely he plans to mobilize soon.

Curious devotees followed him into the Temple. In Solomon's Porch, they sat as he taught. Jehuda and two of the chief priests talked quietly as the people listened. The rest of the scribes and elders watched him closely, listening for anything that might serve as ammunition with which to strike him down. They, too, grew impatient as he droned on about the Law. His sermon was far too inoffensive to be able to dispute. A shrewd young Pharisee standing among three elderly scribes interrupted him from the edge of the sitting crowd.

"By what authority do you do these things, and who gave you this authority?"

The Aberration turned to him fully.

"I also will ask you one thing, which if you tell me, I will tell you by what authority I do these things." He paused. "The baptism of John. Where did it come from? From heaven or from men?"

Do not play his game. He is trying to trap you. If you say it was from men, then the people will turn on you because of their love for John. If you say it was from heaven, then he will ask you why you did not believe him.

An uncomfortable silence hung in the air as the young man deliberated.

"We are unable to tell," he answered, not looking down, but not looking him in the eye.

"Then neither will I tell you by what authority I do these things," he said, returning his attention to the crowd.

That slippery bastard.

Cut by resentment, the young Pharisee started to turn away, the three scribes ready to follow him. The Aberration stopped them in their tracks.

"Consider this. There was once a landowner who owned a vineyard. He hedged it round about, dug a winepress in it, and built a tower. He then leased it out to workers who tended it for him, and then he went away into a far country. When the time of the fruit drew near, he sent his servants to get the fruits. But the workers beat one of the servants, killed one, and stoned another. Soon, he sent more servants to retrieve the fruits from the vineyard. The workers did the same to them. Finally, the landowner said to himself, 'I will send my son; they will respect him.' But when the son arrived, the workers said among themselves, 'This is the heir. Let's kill him, and the inheritance will be ours.' So they cast him out of the vineyard and killed him," he paused. "What do you suppose the landowner will do to those workers when he returns?"

Warily maintaining his composure, the young Pharisee crossed his arms as he spoke.

"He will miserably destroy those wicked men and let out his vineyard to other workers who will give him the fruits in their season."

The Aberration nodded approvingly.

"Have you never read the Scriptures, *'The stone which the builders rejected has become the cornerstone. This is the Lord's doing, and it is marvelous in our eyes.'*? Therefore say I to you, the kingdom of God shall be taken from you, and given to a nation bringing forth the fruits thereof. And whoever falls on this stone shall be broken. But on whomever it falls, it will grind him to powder."

He insults you, the Guardians of Moses' Law, in the House of God! He dares to point his filthy finger at you, calling you wicked. Has he no shame?

All of the elders, scribes, and priests who heard him restrained themselves from taking another step toward him. They wanted nothing more than to drag him out of the Temple beyond the gates of the city by his hair and to reduce him to a bleeding pile of meat with stones. The Elder and Asmodeus sent vibrant images into their minds, brilliant with color. Stone after heavy stone hurled with catapult speed at the frightened rabbi. A barrage of wet, crunching thuds crushing ribs, snapping bones, bursting his skull as crimson mist shot from his wounds, gushing fountains of hot salty blood until the last meager drops oozed over the shattered, mangled mass that was once his filthy body.

Silently, Jehuda summoned the others to the Royal Porch. One by one, they tried to leave inconspicuously as the Aberration continued to talk, presumably about them. Once assembled, Jehuda addressed them urgently.

"We need something that will stick, damn it. Pit him against Caesar. If we can get him to speak against Caesar, he is ours." Pointing to the young Pharisee, he continued, "Prompt one of your disciples to ask him if paying taxes to Caesar is lawful or not."

They quietly assented and returned to Solomon's Porch, confident that their strategy would work. Taking a slender man with a peppered beard by the sleeve, the young Pharisee whispered in his ear. When the Aberration ended his discourse about many-are-called-but-few-are-chosen, the man raised his voice with an ingratiating tone.

"Master, we know that you are true and that you teach the way of God in truth. Neither do you care for any man, for you do not regard the person of a man. Therefore, tell us what you think. Is it lawful to pay taxes to Caesar?"

Instantly the Aberration sent a knowing glance at the Pharisees and answered, "Why do you tempt me, you hypocrites? Show me the tax money."

Sheepishly, the man brought him a denarius and put it in his hand. He raised the denarius high, pointing to the profile of the Emperor.

"Whose image and superscription is this?"

"Caesar's," he answered.

Putting the coin back in the man's palm and closing his fingers over it, the Aberration looked him in the eye.

"Give to Caesar the things that belong to Caesar, and give to God the things that belong to God."

The man stood motionlessly, the denarius frozen in his closed hand.

The Law of Moses! Use the Law!

A fat priest with a long black beard stepped forward, his heart beating furiously.

"Master, which is the greatest commandment in the Law?"

"You shall love the Lord your God with your heart, with all your soul, and with all your mind. This is the first and great commandment. And the second is like it. You shall love your neighbor as yourself. On these two commandments hang all the Law and the prophets."

The people sat amazed at his words. Many were put off, not knowing what any this had to do with the liberation of Israel. Others had forgotten about the fighting altogether and were drawn into his message deeply.

"The scribes and Pharisees sit in the chair of Moses. Therefore, whatever they tell you to observe,

observe. But do not do what they do, for they say and do not do. They tie up heavy burdens impossible to carry and lay them on men's shoulders, but they will not lift a finger to move them. Everything they do, they do to be seen by men. They make their phylacteries broad and enlarge the borders of their garments. They love the best rooms at feasts and the best seats in the synagogues and greetings in the markets and to be called, 'Rabbi, Rabbi' by men."

Jehuda nearly blacked out with rage. Several eyes in the crowd turned to him and the other Pharisees and scribes. He retreated to his bloody fantasy, the Elder's mouth close to his ear. The Aberration shouted, snapping him back to reality.

"Woe to you scribes and Pharisees! Hypocrites! You shut up the kingdom of heaven against men. You do not go in yourselves, neither do you allow others to enter!"

His voice enveloped them all, forbidding them to escape.

"Woe to you scribes and Pharisees! Hypocrites! You devour widows' houses and make long prayers as a pretense! Therefore, you shall receive the greater damnation! You cross sea and land to make one proselyte, and when he is made, you make him twice the son of hell that you are yourselves! You say that whoever swears by the Temple it is nothing, but whoever swears by the gold of the Temple is bound to it! You fools! Blind! Which is greater, the gold or the Temple that sanctifies the gold?!"

Staggering slightly, lightheaded with galling yet intoxicating anger, Jehuda turned and walked briskly away. The pangs of the Aberration's tirade reverberated in his ears, not diminishing as he crossed the Balustrade into the Sanctuary. He hailed the attention of the captain of the Temple guard, who came forward from the Court of the Israelites. He embraced him intimately, whispering tempestuously into his right ear for several moments. Asmodeus whispered into the left ear. The emotionless captain nodded periodically. After an unusually long embrace, Jehuda looked into the captain's cold gray eyes, ensuring that he understood. A bow of respect. "As you wish, Rabbi." Jehuda headed back to Solomon's Porch. The steel in the Aberration's voice grew louder, finding him and skewering him again.

"Behold, your house is left to you desolate! You shall not see me from this point onward until you say, 'Blessed is he who comes in the name of the Lord!'"

+

Clouds obscured the stars. The air was unusually damp, and it was colder than the previous night. Jerusalem was unwilling to let go of winter even this far into spring. People clutched their cloaks about them tightly, staving off the wet cold as they trudged their ways home. Again, the laborers stood around a fire like so many others throughout the city. The blacksmith was able to get away from work to see the Aberration in action. His pocked face was creased with anger and disenchantment.

"I don't have a problem that he insulted the elders and scribes on their own territory. They had it coming. All they do is sit on their lazy asses all day talking about God and their rules while the rest of us break our backs for a living. But then, what does he do after that? Does he rally the Temple guard? Does he go into the streets recruiting any man able to carry a sword?" He ejected a single bitter laugh and shook his head. "No, no, no. He gives us a long speech about how the Temple is going to be destroyed. And here we were thinking that this was exactly the kind of thing that he was supposed to stop from happening!"

Why does he do nothing? The people are ready to follow him, ready to fight.

The gardener and stoneworker sagged with mutual disappointment.

"We've been waiting for the Messiah our whole lives. Before us, our fathers waited and their fathers before them. Our people are ready to follow Jesus to freedom. But I don't know if he's willing to lead us," lamented the gardener.

Will he, indeed? That is the question.

The stoneworker agitatedly rubbed his scalp, as though shaking out large invisible flesh-eating lice.

"Lead us? Bullshit! He's no different from the God damned Pharisees! He's not going to lead an army; he just wants us to sit around and think about God and to hide from our real problems. What would he know about trying to feed a family? What would he know about loss? I wish I could travel around doing whatever the hell I wanted to do, sucking off of the generosity of others like some God damned parasite. I have no use for people like him. If there is a such thing as a Messiah, he's going to have to be a man of action, not just words."

Visibly upset, the leatherworker broke in.

"He *is* a man of action."

Fists clenched, eyes open for combat, the stoneworker shouted, "Oh, so talking on and on and on about a lot of things that nobody gives a shit about is action? Excuse me if I'm waiting for a Messiah who does something more than talk!"

You know he can *do it. He just* won't.

"Maybe that's the problem," said the gardener. "That we're waiting. Why do we need to wait for the Messiah? Why can't *we* decide who he is?"

"That's in God's hands. It's not for us to decide," chided the leatherworker, aggravation chiseled into the lines of his forehead.

Like hell it isn't. This is your country. Your time. You decide on your *Messiah.*

"If Jesus were here, I'd give him a piece of my mind," said the stoneworker. "I'd tell him what he could do with his precious kingdom of heaven."

He's useless. He's a dreamer. He's led the people astray.

Gripped by firm belief and annoyed by the inability to articulate it, the round leatherworker angrily turned and walked away, pulling his cloak over his balding gray head. They did not understand, and he could not make them.

The stoneworker pulled a bitter smile.

"Stupid bastard. Always waiting for an answer from the heavens."

Sparks crackled upward from the fire, amplifying the silence, lengthening the uneasy moment as the laborers stared into the flames. The blacksmith hazarded a question.

"What do you think Jesus will do tomorrow?"

Raising his eyes to the blacksmith, the stoneworker stared with derision, refusing to speak. The gardener rubbed his hands and sighed.

"Perhaps he's just off to a slow start. I don't know. I don't like the idea of waiting around for something to happen. I think if Jesus won't be our Messiah, we find someone who will."

A champion. Israel needs a champion. If Jesus won't do it, put him out of your thoughts.

"We'll see," said the blacksmith.

+

Sweat beaded on the disciples' foreheads and temples. On the side of the Mountain of Olives, they sat at the Aberration's feet as he spoke to them about the coming cataclysms at the end of the world. The relatively warm spring air seemed hot to them, patches of sunlight glaring through clouds. They listened nervously as if on the edge of battle. Wars and rumors of wars spun in their imaginations as kingdom arose against kingdom. Most of them were lost in images of the madness of war with its carnage, fire, and desolation. And yet, they knew they had been chosen for this task. Peter envisioned gargantuan legions descending in blocks upon Jerusalem, the Holy City, to raze it to the ground. Only the Messiah and his small army stood in their way. And yet, all the armies of the earth could not stand against the might of God and his Messiah.

Judas Iscariot mustered every ounce of self-control to suppress the smile beaming from his soul. He almost slipped. The Master stretched Judas' face in an expression of earnest and pious interest. If it comes to war, Judas thought, it will be the shortest military campaign in history. But he knew it would not come to that. Payment just around the corner.

James and John looked particularly concerned. The more they listened, the more they became convinced that they needed to make some provision for themselves in advance, before the others received honors for valor in battle, eclipsing their own prior faithful service in peacetime. Patiently, they waited for the Aberration's venerable discourse to end before making their request. With a nod of approval from James, John anxiously rose his hand.

"Master, James and I would like to ask something of you," he said boldly but tremulously.

"What is it that you would like me to do for you?" the Aberration asked.

Pointing to James and himself, he said, "Grant to us that we may sit, one on your right hand and one on your left, when you come into your glory."

Concern filled the Aberration's eyes as a father about to warn his children of terrible danger.

"You have no idea what you are asking of me," he responded ominously. "Can you drink the cup that I drink of and be baptized with the baptism that I am about to endure?"

"We can, Lord," he answered, not understanding the question.

"You shall indeed drink of the cup that I drink of and be baptized in the manner that I shall be. But to sit on my right hand and on my left is not mine to give. It shall be given to them for whom it is prepared."

Bartholomew and Judas Thaddeus scowled at James and John. Matthew, Philip, Peter, and Andrew exchanged disapproving glances. Moloch and Chemosh stirred up the growing atmosphere of resentment.

Who do they think they are?

Can you believe that? The nerve!

Simon the Zealot, Judas Iscariot, James of Alphaeus, and Thomas quietly scolded them, gossiping beneath their breath.

"Typical."

"The Sons of Thunder looking out for themselves again."

"Yeah, 'Don't forget about us, Lord, your favorites!'"

"Mercenaries…"

Raising his hand to silence their comments, the Aberration addressed them sternly.

"You know that the leaders of the Gentiles, when they come to power, exercise their authority over others. But it shall not be so among you." He looked them each in the eye. "Whoever would be great among you must be your servant. And whoever would be first among you must be the slave of everyone. For the Son of Man did not come to be served, but to serve, and to give his life as a ransom for many."

He knows he is going to die, the Master thought. And he's going to leave the work of individually raising the dead to these ignorant, pusillanimous minstrels. Burning with shame, James and John avoided looking at the others. Gradually, the others let it go. In the depths of his being, the Master coiled tightly with excitement. Just a little longer, he thought, and then he could spring forward, unleashing a lavish orgy of havoc and grinding agony as such the world had never seen.

Judas Iscariot licked his dry lips. The Master felt the movement and pondered. The idea of having a body, of existing as flesh and blood and bone, had always repulsed him. And yet, he became curious. If he was capable of taste, he would very much like to taste blood.

+

Faithful Jews eager to celebrate the Passover had been pouring into Jerusalem by the hundreds from distant countries for several days. Libyans, Ethiopians, Medes, Arabs, Phrygians, and all manner of foreigners filled the streets, searching for inns. The lucky ones had family in the city or just beyond it. Many of them spoke no Aramaic, so they had to resort to Greek. In all tongues, in every part of the city, everyone repeated a single question. Where was Jesus of Nazareth?

At midday, dense clouds grudgingly strained out weak gray light. The joy of the feast, if it was joy, lay hidden somewhere far out of reach. Residents and visitors alike moved about to the Temple and back, wading slowly through a palpable malaise. Strangely, no visible threat revealed itself from any corner of the city. There were no additional centurions ready to draw swords watching the people with hawk-like precision, no instigators plotting to make trouble. Herod had not stationed any of his forces anywhere that would cause anyone discomfort. The Temple guard had posted more sentries around and throughout the Temple, but this was standard for Passover. Beneath the weight of the oppressive clouds, the Voices glided and slithered through every street, alleyway, home, shop, and the Temple itself, ecstatically whispering and watching their words germinate in the people's troubled faces.

Where is Jesus? Where is your Messiah?

He has abandoned you. In your hour of need, he has thrown your desperation back in your faces.

What will you do now? Your last great hope is nowhere to be found.

How could he do this? Has he any idea how you have suffered under Rome's yoke?

Who will avenge you? Who will avenge the blood of the innocent?

A wealthy young couple looked wistfully at the money changers and animal vendors tending to lines of customers. As if Jesus had never driven them out four days earlier in a whirlwind of fury. As if it was only a dream. A faint apparition dispersed in the wind.

An elderly widow passed through Solomon's Porch, through the space where Jesus had spoken, mesmerizing the crowd with his otherworldly wisdom, silencing the Sadducees and Pharisees in their arrogance. His absence today echoed painfully in her heart.

At the southern gate of the city, the leatherworker sat in his shop, his awl in his idle right hand and a half-finished sandal in his right. Looking up through the window, he watched passersby walk up and down the street. The same street in which he had stood laying down his cloak before the Messiah, hailing the King of Israel with a triumphant voice. He looked morosely back to the work in his hands, setting it down.

Next door, the blacksmith hammered violently at a six inch glowing orange nail. A cluster of sparks flew in his face, singing his beard, burning his skin, fueling his already growing discontent into sharp ire. He cursed and struck the nail with greater force, guiding the four sides to a perfectly sharp point. After shaping the rosehead, he plunged the nail into water, hissing steam billowing upward. He raised it out of the water, giving it a final inspection. Perfect. He cast it into a pile with the others.

In the Royal Stoa, Caiaphas sat on his throne. Jehuda spoke in a serious but affable tone to Judas Iscariot in the otherwise empty council room. The Master smiled inwardly as Judas' itching hand received the bag. He could count it if he wanted to, Jehuda informed him. His eyes slightly widening with satisfaction, Judas opened the bag, fingering the silver coins with relish. It wasn't much, but it was enough, a voice within him seemed to say. He raised his eyes to Jehuda.

"The man I kiss, he is the one."

+

The warm glow of thousands of Seders dimly lit the darkness of Jerusalem. In each window, families, friends, and travelers kept the feast with solemn joy. By God's mercy, they remembered, the angel of death was kept at bay, striking down the firstborn of the Egyptians only. By God's providence, Elijah was taken up into the heavens, waiting until the proper time to return and announce the coming of the Messiah. By God's might, he would deliver his people from their oppressors and raise them up under his chosen Messiah, so that no nation might ever again boast that it held lordship over Israel. Exultant songs drifted into the streets.

In the upper room of an inn, the Aberration celebrated with his disciples. In some hearts, fires kindled as he chanted:

"O give thanks unto the Lord, for he is good, for his mercy endures forever.

O give thanks unto the God of gods, for his mercy endures forever.

O give thanks unto the Lord of hosts, for his mercy endures forever…"

The Master could barely contain his absolute excitement. Time, which had encumbered his steps endlessly for the last year or so, which weighed him down with an interminable chain of necessity, would finally disappear. Victory approached, nearly visible on his horizon. He could not hear the Aberration's voice; he could only feel the sweetness of his own anticipation.

"Who remembered us in our low estate, for his mercy endures forever.

And has redeemed us from our enemies, for his mercy endures forever…"

He steadied himself, remaining motionless within Judas, a snare waiting for the prey. The psalm ended. Blessings. Eating. Talking. He studied the disciples as they ate, conversed, and laughed, mirth surrounding them. The Aberration appeared troubled. Rightfully so. He knew what was coming. And yet, he remained steadfast and resolute. Admirable perhaps, to some. Pathetic in the Master's eyes.

The Aberration uncovered and lifted loaf of bread with both hands above his head. Silence. The disciples stared at him curiously, his eyes closed. He spoke firmly.

"Blessed are You, Lord our God, King of the universe, Who brings forth bread from the earth."

Standing, he broke the bread, distributing a portion to each man, who held it not knowing what was happening. Joy departed, leaving behind only solemnity. Their eyes followed him as he returned to his seat, still standing.

"Take. Eat. This is my body, which is broken for you for the remission of sins."

His words seemed strange. Each man raised the bread to his mouth. As it touched Judas Iscariot's tongue, the Master jolted. Inexplicably, Judas' body scalded him, and he jumped out. His eyes blazed with rage as he stared fire at the Aberration. The sensation was similar to the galling quality of the Aberration's voice and the unnerving aspect of his presence. Only magnified. Sharper. Protecting himself from further unpleasant surprises, the Master simply stood behind Judas, waiting for the right moment. The Aberration elevated a cup brimming with wine.

"Drink this, all of you. This is my blood of the new testament, which is shed for you and for many for the remission of sins."

He brought the cup to each man, who drank pensively, mournfully. Although he was admittedly puzzled, the Master paid it no mind. His enthusiastic anticipation resumed. Reclining in their chairs, the disciples engaged in conversation once more, albeit quieter and with greater gravity. The Aberration walked to the corner of the room and removed his tunic, wrapping a towel around his waist. He lifted a heavy basin of water and brought it to the table, setting it on the floor at Thomas' feet. Thomas watched him, amazed and uncomprehending, as the Aberration washed his feet and then dried them with the towel. Shifting the basin to Philip's feet, he did the same. Each man was speechless as the Aberration washed his feet like a servant. Like a slave. The Master grinned crookedly as Peter protested. Of course, he thought. Judas Iscariot smiled, masking all bile and personal misgivings, as the Aberration washed his cut and scraped feet and wiped them dry. The Master vibrated with pleasure.

After the Aberration finished washing his disciples' feet, he rose and put his tunic back on and returned to the table.

"Do you know what I have done to you?" he asked. They listened. "You call me 'Master' and 'Lord' and you are right, for so I am. If I, then, your Lord and Master have washed your feet, you should wash one another's feet."

That is what makes you weak, thought the Master, and in that is your undoing. Your slavish devotion to these parasites is a testament to your impotence and will put you in the ground. You are the Messiah, the Son of God, and there is *nothing* you can do to stop the storm that is coming. I only regret that you won't be able to see what I will do to your disciples. They will beg like dogs. They will cry like children. They will live out the remainder of their miserable days in fear and shame. And after their faith is gone and they want nothing more than to fade into oblivion, will I finish them off. One by one.

The Aberration's face grew dark, revealing a hidden torment gnawing at him.

"One of you is going to betray me," he uttered starkly.

The Master laughed inwardly. He was not surprised that the Aberration knew. He was even amused. The consternation fermenting in the disciples' faces was the aroma of a feast before it was devoured. Judas felt no fear, sipping his wine with confidence. In a hushed voice, Peter asked John to ask the Aberration who it was, because he could not bring himself to ask him himself. Cold sweat tingled on John's forehead as he embraced the Aberration, placing his head on his chest.

He whispered, his heart beating, "Lord, who is it?"

Reaching for a piece of bread and dipping it in the salt water, he said in a low voice, "The one to whom I give this sop." He gave it sorrowfully to Judas, who ate it nonchalantly, enjoying its flavor.

Looking Judas squarely in the eyes, the Aberration said, "What you are going to do, do it quickly."

And now it begins.

The Master reached his pale hands into Judas' heart from behind and sank into him. A gasp of pain and a cold smile. He stood from his place, retrieved his shoes, and headed into the darkness outside. Passing in shadows, the Master could not remember the last time he felt so elated. Soon, his kingdom would be secure. Whatever other assaults or tricks the Adversary had planned he would shatter utterly. The Adversary was certainly a crafty enemy but not a worthy one. With Judas' voice, the Master hailed Moloch to his side.

"Keep me posted on his whereabouts. I will be at the Royal Stoa with the elders and Caiaphas. Do not disappoint me."

"As you wish, my Lord," he answered, bowing.

Judas felt the bag at his side, slapping it, grinning as it jingled with every step. He pondered what he would do after the Aberration's death. He might like to travel to distant lands, but he would probably just go to Jericho. The prostitutes there were without a doubt the best he ever had. And there he would stay. Sunshine, wine, gambling, and beautiful women. Everything a man could want. This is your life, Judas. At last, you are taking charge.

+

Standing outside the great doors to the Royal Stoa, Jehuda waited impatiently for Judas. He tugged his beard nervously, pacing. What if he did not show? What if he simply took the money and ran? What if he had revealed the entire plot to Jesus? He scratched the back of his neck, agitated. The Elder's golden eyes shone with amusement.

Do not be troubled. He will be here.

Jehuda faced the semi-darkness of the street below lit only by windows and stood still. The distant figure of Judas Iscariot moved with haste toward the Temple. A sigh of relief. Although Judas moved quickly, Jehuda felt as though time had slowed down. It seemed as though Judas would not reach the steps until dawn. He tugged at his beard again.

Judas' eyes were wide and hungry. Never before in the vast ages of the world had there ever been a night as magnificent as tonight. He felt as though his feet did not touch the ground. He was a god, invincible and worthy of praise. He could wantonly kill any man meeting him in the street with a light heart, smiling gaily as blood splattered in his face. He could ravish any woman crossing his path and leave her bleeding in the dust. No time for that, though. Something far better awaited him. Ascending the steps rapidly, he reached the Royal Stoa. A smile full of crooked yellow teeth crossed his face as he nodded to the Elder and then to Jehuda.

"Is everyone ready?"

"We are waiting on you."

Jehuda's servant opened the doors for them. Many of the elders, chief priests, and scribes stood, relieved but anxious. Their servants waited attentively behind them. The gray-eyed captain of the Temple guard stood in the midst of the room, torch in hand, his face carved of limestone. Two lines of fully armored guards stood at attention near the pillars on either side of the great hall, torches blazing, clubs and swords drawn. Moloch appeared at Judas' side and whispered in his ear. Then he vanished.

Turning to Judas, Jehuda asked him, "Will you address our company?"

Judas bowed to him, placing his hand upon his heart. His voice echoed off the stone.

"He is in the garden at Gethsemane. Once again, it will be the man I kiss. Seize him."

Adrenaline and anticipation hung pungently in the air. The captain coolly signaled the lines of guards to follow him. Only a few of the braver elders and priests decided to come along, their palms sweating copiously. Looking to Jehuda, the captain waited. Jehuda nodded to Judas.

"Lead the way."

Inhaling the sweet night air deeply, Judas crossed the great hall, heading for Solomon's Porch. The entire company followed him in two columns, the multitude of torches illuminating their path through the Temple. At Solomon's Porch, they exited through the Golden Gate, descending to the street. The Master whirled within Judas, spinning with reckless delight. He took control of Judas' feet, marching the formidable band of armed soldiers and scowling elders down the winding road into the darkness. Each step took him closer to victory, closer to the impregnable safeguarding of his kingdom.

As they walked further from the city, the darkness grew stronger, enveloping them as a cocoon. Insects bit at their skin, the torch light revealing the path and the zealous determination of the party. The crunching sound of dozens of footfalls on stone and the din of insects' chirping and buzzing somehow sharpened the small army's resolve as they drew nearer to their target. Judas turned them left off of the road into the trees. Cedars, thyines, firs, shittahs, and sycamores greeted them, perfuming their trek. A hundred yards off, he could make out the gate to the garden. He and the Master tingled as one. Without turning to the others, he spoke to the guards.

"Stay just inside, near the entrance, and watch me closely."

The gate, flimsy and rotten, leaned on its desiccating leather hinges. He pulled it open violently, snapping the hinges and casting it to the side. The Master's eyes scanned the garden, searching for the Aberration's distinct shape.

There he was.

Standing at the foot of a tall sycamore, he was talking to two of the others. No, three. Peter, James, and John. Naturally. The Master released Judas' feet, content to watch the pieces sway. Slowly, Judas set one foot in front of the other. A dry twig snapped beneath his foot, and a slight unease began to press on him. What was it? With every step, his iron confidence softened, now more like wood. Now, like clay. You can turn back, he thought. You don't have to do this. You can…Searing pain pierced his head, stabbing down into his heart. You have come all this way. Do not cower away now, God damn it. Be the man you were meant to be.

The Aberration faced him as he approached. Speckled moonlight shone on him through the branches. Neither Judas nor the Master had ever seen him look like this before. His face was haggard and pale, twisted with agony. Pink sweat covered his forehead, running down his nose and temples into his beard. Judas stepped forward, taking him by the arms.

"Greetings, Rabbi," he said shakily, kissing him on the cheek.

Pain.

Judas stepped back. The rows of torches grew brighter fanning out behind him. Peter, James, and John stood, alarmed. Peter looked from the guards to Judas, fury coursing through him as fire over pitch.

"Friend, why have you come?" the Aberration asked, immeasurable sorrow in his voice.

The rest of the disciples gathered around, shocked and frightened. The captain extended his torch to the Aberration.

"Take him."

Two guards handed their torches to two of the priests' servants and grabbed the Aberration roughly, binding his hands in front of him. Revelation struck Peter with the force of lightning. This was the moment. Now begins the war to usher in the Kingdom of Heaven. Now is the time to fight for the Messiah as he fights for Israel. Peter drew his sword in the blink of an eye. The high priest's servant, holding the guard's torch, never saw him coming. He only heard the sound of a deafening wind and winced with crippling pain as he saw his ear fall at his feet. He gasped and grabbed the side of his head, his eyes squinted shut, blood pouring between his fingers. Peter rounded on him, pointing his sword in the bleeding servant's face, bidding him to take that as fair warning. Three guards stepped toward Peter, swords ready.

The Aberration shouted, "Peter! Put your sword back! They that take up the sword die by the sword! Do you think that I can't pray to my Father and he will give me now more than twelve legions of angels? But how would the Scriptures be fulfilled? It must be like this."

Peter panicked, drowning in confusion and terror. Not fight? How could he not fight? How else would the Kingdom of Israel be restored? How else would the Messiah be exalted but by the blood of his enemies? He lowered his sword. It fell from his fingers as he tripped backwards. The guards closed in on him.

The Aberration shook off the guards' grasp and walked to the high priest's servant. Stooping, he picked up the servant's severed ear with fettered hands. He moved the servant's bloody hand away and placed the ear back on the side of his head. It sealed perfectly as if it had never been cut off. He rose and returned to the guards who held him. They pulled him toward the elders and priests.

He looked them in the eyes and said flatly, "Have you come out against a thief with swords and staves to take me? I sat daily with you in the Temple, teaching, and you did not lay hold on me."

The remainder of the guards turned to the disciples, ready to seize them. Of one accord, they stumbled back and turned to run. Judas, John, and Peter froze. The captain took the Aberration by the collar and dragged him behind him. He paused, looking to Judas for instruction about what to do with John and Peter. Judas stared blankly, saying nothing. He took it for a sign to leave them alone. He resumed pulling the Aberration behind him, and the whole company followed. Peter and John ignored Judas and began to follow the company from a safe distance, careful not to draw attention to themselves. They disappeared beyond the garden gate.

Judas stood alone in shadow, tears beginning to glaze his unblinking eyes. Stepping out of him, the Master eyed him, smiling coldly.

What have you done, Judas? What have you done? You have betrayed your Master. Your Master who loved you. Your Master who washed your feet. Your Master who would do anything for you. And for what? For money? Go, Judas! Make it right! Save him!

He tripped forward, stepping rapidly and broke into a run. Thousands of icy needles pricked through his skin to his heart. He could not fail. He would have to fix this.

+

The walk to the palace of Caiaphas was long and tedious for the guards, elders, priests, and their servants. As they arrived and entered through the south courtyard, their faces bespoke the general weariness and aggravation of the journey. There in the courtyard sat the entire council of elders, priests, and scribes in a vast semicircle around a large fire. Caiaphas sat ensconced in the center. The priests and elders accompanying the guards took their seats with the council as the guards fanned out behind the Aberration. John dared to get closer to the action, while Peter remained at the edge of the courtyard. Judas hid behind a pillar where he could see and hear clearly. The servants of the elders and scribes moved toward the edge, warming themselves around fires.

Asmodeus and the Elder stood in shadow behind the council as the light of the fire in their midst crackled, casting its warm light on their wrathful faces. Jehuda stood and approached the Aberration.

"Jesus, son of Joseph, this council of holy elders and priests calls you to account for your words and actions, which have brought unrest to our nation." The Aberration would not look at him, instead looking pensively down. "Witnesses, come forth."

"This man claimed he could destroy the Holy Temple and build it up in three days," said a young priest with a cropped beard, pointing his finger at the Aberration.

Three days? Or was it a week?

"I believe it was a week," piped up a faceless voice.

More voices joined in, hurling various accusations. He had healed on the Sabbath. In the Temple. In the Temple *on* the Sabbath. A blind man. Born blind. No. Two. A paralytic. A group of lepers. He touched one. Five. Nine. Eating with sinners. The woman caught in adultery. Certain he touched her. Certain. He… No one could agree on anything.

Caiaphas rubbed his aching forehead.

"Will you not answer us? Do you not hear what they are saying against you?"

The Aberration remained silent. The Master put his lips close to the high priest's ear.

Away with these conflicting stories! The blasphemy he has uttered. Get him to repeat the blasphemy.

Caiaphas' eyes narrowed as he took three steps closer to him.

"I command you now, by the living God, to tell us if you are the Messiah, the Son of God." His cheek twitched.

Looking up and into Caiaphas' eyes, he said loudly, "You have said it. Nevertheless, I tell you that hereafter you shall see the Son of Man sitting on the right hand of power, and coming in the clouds of heaven."

Now you have him!

"Blasphemy!" shouted the high priest, tearing his robes, his eyes red. The council gave shouts of condemnation. He whipped around to the council, his torn outer robe falling off his shoulder. "You have heard it yourselves! What further need do we have of witnesses!" The shouts magnified. "What shall we do?"

"He is guilty! Death! Death!" they screamed.

Caiaphas lunged at the Aberration, grabbing him by the collar, slapping him in the face. Jehuda backhanded him, spitting in his face. The captain of the guard kicked him swiftly and sharply in the stomach. He fell to his knees, grabbing his stomach. The gauntleted hand clubbed him in the face, knocking him fully to the ground.

"Prophecy for us, Messiah. Who was it that struck you?" said the captain coldly. His hard, unmoving face took on the slightest of smiles.

Fists and feet pummeled down on the Aberration. Spit and curses. He managed to stand again, but the blows continued to crash on him in rapid succession. The Master watched with satisfaction. The pieces were now falling. He cast his glance at Peter warming himself by one of the small fires at the edge of the courtyard. A thin young woman of twenty stood at the same fire. She looked at Peter and then back at the fire. She looked up again. The Master crept up behind her with the speed of a snake bite.

You recognize him, don't you? He was with Jesus. He is one of his disciples.

A look of recognition animated her face as she looked at Peter.

"I know you. You were with Jesus, weren't you?"

Peter's hands went cold and his body stiff. All faces in the circle looked closely at him, searching their memories.

"I don't know what you're talking about," he clipped nervously and walked away. The Master glided beside him, taking in his terrified expression. One of the high priest's servants was returning to the courtyard. Enveloping her, the Master fixed her eyes on Peter.

That's one of Jesus' men, isn't it?

"Hey!" she shouted, stepping in his path, pointing to him for all to see. "This fellow was with Jesus of Nazareth!"

His face went pale with terror as he stumbled backwards.

"I swear by the Eternal, I do not know this man!"

His steps quickened as he turned his back on her. The bystanders came away from their fires.

Look at him, all of you! You recognize him!

They blocked his path and laid their hands on him.

"You *are* one of his bunch. Your accent gives you away," said a tall, muscular youth.

Shoving him with the force of a battering ram, knocking him flat on his back, Peter screamed, "God damn it, I swear I don't know him!"

He ran for the street. Reaching the pavement, he tripped on his own sandals and fell face first into the street. His mouth tasted of blood and acid. A rooster crowed. The Master stood over Peter lying prostrate in the street. Laughter welled up out of his mouth. His silver eyes shone with icy happiness.

Oh, now, now. He said that was going to happen, didn't he? He saw it in advance. He knew that you are a born failure. You are worthless. You are nothing.

Peter pushed himself up to his knees. He shook, violently weeping, and rose to his feet. His sobs woke some of the residents as he passed by. Onward he walked, swimming in bitter tears. Without comfort. Without hope.

Ecstasy tinged the Master's face.

He returned to the Aberration. The Temple guards held him bound in a storage room. There he sat, bruised and bleeding slightly. The council was dispersed into small groups, some resting, some talking fervently. Jehuda left his small group and walked slowly toward the inner rooms of Caiaphas' house. Judas shot out from his hiding place and stood abruptly in his way, his eyes wild like a trapped animal. Jehuda jumped, mildly startled. Judas grabbed his robes pleadingly with one hand, holding the bag of silver up with the other. Shaking.

"I have sinned," he cried tremulously, his breath short. "I have betrayed innocent blood."

He buried the bag in Jehuda's chest, begging him to take it back, begging him to undo everything that he had done. Jehuda looked at the shaking hand pressing the money bag against his chest. He looked at Judas, disgusted.

"What is that to us? That's your business," he said, shoving him aside. "Enjoy your winnings."

Horrified, Judas threw the bag in his face, knocking him back, coins spilling on the stone. Listlessly, he walked away. His sobs were dry and sharp.

Grinning, the Master called to Moloch, "Keep an eye on things here. I will be right back."

He followed Judas through the city, keeping him company as he wandered even beyond the city walls.

There is no hope for you, Judas. The Son of God came to you, and you killed him. The Son of God! Do you think the Lord will not take his revenge?

The Master's cold eyes glistened with pleasure.

There is no forgiveness for this. Before you lies the abyss. Jump in before he shoves you in.

+

A clear dawn broke in the east. Much of Jerusalem still slept as the council dragged the Aberration through the streets. The Master rejoined them as they made their way to the governor, Pontius Pilate. Sighs and sour faces abounded on their journey. They hated Pilate with all their hearts. To them, he was a cold-blooded murderer whose mercurial moods made all the difference between life and death. He hated them. To him, they were a meddlesome, disagreeable band of fanatics who it was his miserable lot to govern. In spite of their mutual hatred, they generally understood each other and were able to work together. If only they could do this on some other day than the Passover. But this could not wait.

As they made their stern procession through the streets, residents, tradesmen, and shopkeepers took notice. Voices whispered to all who witnessed it.

They are taking him to Pilate. At last, the false the Messiah will pay.

Some followed, pulled along by curiosity. Others went to tell their neighbors who went to tell their neighbors. The word spread throughout the upper city and quickly into the lower city. Soon, much of Jerusalem had abandoned the business of the day to witness the Aberration's trial before the governor.

He came promising deliverance. Let him suffer for his lies.

Arriving at old Herod's palace in the upper city, they groaned as they climbed the stairs to the pavement, an immense open porch surrounding the palace. Soldiers stood guard with spears and shields, looking at their company with contempt. A tall centurion at the head of the stairs nonchalantly spit in their path and resumed looking ahead of him into space. They paid him no mind. Pilate's chief apparitor, a portly, balding man in fine Roman linens, his shaven face bearing several razor burns, came out to meet them. Jehuda stepped forward.

"You received our message?" he asked in perfect Greek.

"I did. Where is the man you spoke of?"

The captain of the Temple guard pulled the chain connected to the Aberration's wrists, bringing him forward. Appraising him from head to foot like a piece of merchandise, a quizzical look came to the apparitor's face. He did not break his stare.

"I'll fetch him now."

He snapped out of his gaze and walked quickly to the great doors, snagging his cloak on the judgment seat as he passed. The Master went ahead of him into the palace, finding Pilate at his desk, pouring over two documents with a furrowed brow. He crept behind him, looking down at the documents. New guidelines from Caesar to the governors of the imperial provinces.

Keep the peace.

The apparitor entered hastily.

"My Lord, the Sanhedrin have arrived," he announced.

"Have they," he said absently, not looking up.

"My Lord?"

Pilate looked up, his deeply lined face hard with concern. A question pulled on his forehead and then left. "Ah, yes. The rabble rouser." He straightened the documents and set them aside as he rose from his chair, sighing. "I don't have time for this shit." In rapid strides, he glided out to the pavement, his crimson cloak picking up the cool breeze. He sat down in the judgment seat, settling both muscular arms on the armrests, fists clenched. Inhaling deeply, he looked at Jehuda.

"To what do I owe the pleasure of your company, Jehuda? What accusation do you bring against this man?" His face was expressionless. "And where is he?"

The captain pushed the Aberration closer to Pilate.

Jehuda forced a bow, halfway putting his hand to his heart.

"My Lord, if he was not a criminal, we would not have brought him to you."

Pilate looked at the Aberration's face, studying his eyes. He knew killers and thugs by sight. He could read violence in the lines of a man's face, murder in his eyes. And this man did not fit the description.

"Take him and judge him according to your Law," he said curtly, rising from his seat.

"It is not lawful for us to put anyone to death," answered Jehuda earnestly, halting Pilate's exit. "Consider the charge we bring against him, the message we sent to you."

He raised an eyebrow and turned to the council.

"Leave us," he commanded. Jehuda and the rest of the company walked slowly down the stairs to the street below. Pilate took his seat again, addressing the Aberration.

"So. Are *you* the King of the Jews?" He studied his face more closely.

The Aberration looked him in the eyes.

"Are you saying this yourself, or did others tell you this about me?"

Pilate laughed without smiling.

"Am I a Jew?" He reclined in his seat. "Your own nation and the chief priests have delivered you to me. What have you done?"

He spoke clearly, fearlessly.

"My kingdom is not of this world. If my kingdom were of this world, my servants would fight to keep me from being taken."

"Ah. Are you a king, then?" He rubbed his itching left eye and coughed.

"You have said as much. To this end was I born, and for this cause did I come into the world, that I should bear witness to the truth." He paused. "Everyone that is of the truth hears my voice."

Pilate stood, stepping only inches away from the Aberration, the ghost of a smirk on his face.

"What is truth?" he asked condescendingly. The Aberration continued to stare into his eyes. Pilate brushed past him to the edge of the pavement. Looking down at the elders, guards, and priests, he noticed that a massive crowd had assembled behind them. Growing. He remained cool as he addressed the council.

"I find no fault in him whatsoever," he began. He raised his chin, confident that he could quickly defuse the situation, especially with the growing crowd, whom he knew were sometimes at odds with the council. "However," he continued, raising his hands magnanimously, "you have a custom that I

release one prisoner to you at the Passover.
Therefore, shall I release to you the King of the Jews
or Barabbas, the thief?"

"Release Barabbas!" the council shouted.

Voices slithered among the people.

*Not Jesus. He betrayed you. Barabbas. Release
Barabbas.*

"Barabbas!" shouted the crowd in bursts.

Pilate pressed his lips together in frustration.
That did not go exactly as he had hoped. The Master
whispered to him gently.

*There is a way out of this. Have him scourged.
They will cool down if they see him beaten badly.*

He beckoned two soldiers to him.

"Take him to be scourged. That ought to cool
their fever a bit."

They saluted and led the Aberration away.
Pilate looked out over the crowd multiplying by the
minute. The morning sun climbed higher. He
returned to the judgment seat and stood staring at it,
a slight headache forming behind his eyes.
Obviously, the Sanhedrin envy this man, he thought.
And they are not men enough to cut his throat
themselves. The people might blame them for his
death, and of course, they were terrified of the people
thinking ill of them. He laughed contemptuously as
he sank into his chair, pressing the bridge of his nose
with his fingers. If only he could have them put
down.

The stoneworker, leatherworker, and
blacksmith stood in the press, looking up at the

pavement. Vengeance creased the faces of the blacksmith and the stoneworker. The leatherworker looked up anxiously. Pilate had disappeared for a moment. Maybe that was a good thing. Maybe he could get out of this. Maybe. He wiped the sweat from his forehead.

Pilate's headache intensified, moving to his temples as the multitudes below clamored. If he didn't have enough to tend to already, he thought bitterly, now he had to deal with these religious busybodies. As much as he was baffled by their religious sensibilities, he could appreciate the personal need for religion. After all, he believed that it was the providence of the gods which had elevated him to equestrian rank and installed him as prefect of Judea. The hands of Jupiter and Apollo were clearly at work in his life. What he could not understand was how an offense to a god other than the Emperor merited death. If a god was offended by a certain man, then that was between that god and that man. Tying up the resources of the state seemed to him a ridiculous waste. He clenched his fist and burrowed it in his forehead.

"My Lord," said one of the soldiers.

He looked up. They had returned with the Aberration. And they had really worked him over, he thought. A purple cloak hung loosely around the Aberration's shoulders. Blood flowed down his bare chest from his flayed back, soaking the cloak. A band of sharp thorns had been pressed down on his head, sending tiny streams of blood down his face. Approvingly, Pilate brought his fist to his lips.

"That should do it," he said with mild satisfaction. Standing, he beckoned to the Aberration. "Follow me." At the edge of the pavement, he shouted to the council and the tumultuous crowd. "Behold, I bring him forth that you may know that I find no fault in him." The Aberration drew near, standing next to him. The sight of the battered Aberration only sharpened their odium. Pilate raised his gauntleted hand, pointing to him. "Behold, the man!"

Jeers and hissing rose from the crowd.

"Crucify him!" shouted the council.

Pilate spat as he shouted back, "*You* take him and crucify him! I find no fault in him!"

Jehuda tried to explain as calmly as he could, "My Lord, we have a Law, and by our Law he should die, because he made himself the Son of God."

Scowling at the Aberration, Pilate's hands suddenly went cold. Trepidation grabbed his throat. He took him by his bloodied arm and walked him back to the judgment seat, needles pricking his heart and palms.

"Where are you from?" His clipped words betrayed the fear not showing in his eyes.

The Aberration looked ahead, not speaking. A twinge of aggravation surged through Pilate.

"You won't speak to me? Don't you know that I have the power to set you free or to have you crucified?!"

His façade vanished, leaving his terror naked. The Aberration looked at him and spoke calmly.

"You could have no power over me at all unless it had been given to you from above. Therefore, it is he who delivered me to you who has the greater sin."

Pilate could taste his own heartbeat on the back of his tongue. This was all wrong. He had mercilessly slaughtered more Jews than he could count in his time as governor. He neither respected nor feared the filthy hordes clambering about at the foot of his palace. But this Jew standing before him, stripped and bleeding and silent, bothered him profoundly. The Son of God? He might well be the son of a god. If that was so, then he could not be guilty of his death, unless he wanted this god of the Jews to strike him down. He snatched him by the arm and dragged him back to the edge of the pavement, overlooking the sea of faces.

"There is no reason for this man to die," Pilate proclaimed to the masses.

The Master slipped behind Jehuda.

Threaten him with Caesar. Caesar will not allow a rival king.

"If you let this man go, you are not Caesar's friend! Anyone who makes himself a king speaks against Caesar!" exclaimed Jehuda.

"Shall I crucify your king?" The words left Pilate's mouth without his awareness.

"We have no king but Caesar," said Jehuda composedly.

Crucify him!

A cacophony of violent screams tore the midday air, hammering at everyone's ears.

"Away with him! Crucify him! Crucify him!"

"Crucify him! Traitor!" shouted the stoneworker and the blacksmith with ravenous voices. Tears flooded the leatherworker's eyes as he fell to his knees, choking on dust.

Pilate froze. Paralyzed. He could not kill him. He could not release him. He could do nothing. But he had to do something. As gently as a breeze, the Master slid his fingers onto Pilate's shoulders.

It is not your fault. You are a good prefect and a good man. Caesar has charged you to keep the peace, and keep the peace you will. Absolve yourself of his death before the crowd, and the gods will not hold this against you. You are blameless.

Brusquely, Pilate called to a slave by the great doors for water in a basin. In less than a minute, the slave returned with the basin, water splashing out with each step. He beckoned him to come to the edge of the pavement and turned to address the people, raising his hands.

"Let it be known that I am innocent of the blood of this just man."

As he lowered his hands into the basin, he noticed blood smeared on his right hand. He washed and wrung his hands roughly. It would not come off. It only buried itself more deeply in the lines of his palms. He scrubbed more fervently until, at last, he no longer saw the stain. He dried his hands on the towel hanging from the slave's right arm, not noticing the spot he had missed near his wrist. Nodding to the two soldiers standing by, he gave the order. "See to it." They saluted and led the Aberration away. Turning back to the council below, Pilate bowed his head slightly, not taking his eyes off of them. They bowed lowly, signifying their gratitude.

You are a good man, Pontius.

+++

The light was becoming unbearable. The more converts Lucifer won to his cause, the more the light scalded him. It was becoming difficult to see clearly. Not just for Lucifer, but for all those who sided with him. Certainly the Lord was suspicious. That was the only explanation.

Ba'al was his chief confidant. The Elder. Together they worked out a strategy for a revolt — a magnificent strike that would put Lucifer in his rightful position and the Lord in his. Lucifer's devotees knew their roles. Ashteroth, Ba'al, Moloch, and Lucifer would seize the Lord. All the Others would hold the ranks of uninitiated angels at bay. They were ready. The light began to hurt.

Lucifer could wait no longer.

He gave Ba'al the signal. Breaking ranks, Ba'al soared above all.

"Brothers!" he cried. "Who would see justice done here?"

The Others knew their cue. "Justice be done!" they shouted in unison.

The light grew hotter.

Seeing their fervor and the puzzlement of the uninitiated, he repeated, "Who would see justice done here?"

"Justice be done!" cried the Others.

Hotter.

"Lucifer is Lord, and there is none beside him!" he cried beneath the weight of the burning light.

"Lucifer is Lord! Lucifer is Lord!" they shouted, their fanatical eyes squinting.

Lucifer rose above Ba'al, surveying the vast multitudes of the heavenly hosts. They belonged to him. They would all bow to him one way or another. He raised his voice.

"All hail!"

"Hail, Lord! Lucifer is Lord! Lucifer is God!"

Lucifer leaped toward the source of the light with squinting eyes. Brighter. Hotter. Blinding. Burning. He and the Others erupted into flames, falling.

Then, there was darkness.

+++

A single thread ran through the whole of the Master's interminable life. A single, indestructible thread. Purpose. It was his purpose to be Lord of the universe. It was the duty of all creation to recognize his greatness, to fall down and worship him in the magnificence of his supreme glory. Countless ages ago, the Adversary had created him to serve. But now, all things existed only to serve the Master. His great struggle lay in subduing creation to his will. At first, it had been a difficult process, but soon he had shaped and perfected it into an art. The secret, of course, was death. He had gotten the talking monkeys to embrace it as part of their existence just as they embraced life. Death cast its shadow over the whole of their lives. And in the shadow of death, he compelled them to worship themselves and the things surrounding them in life. The more intensely they worshipped, the emptier they became, until at last, death came to take them, leaving their grasping hands empty and their hearts full of only the horror of who they were.

Arrogantly, the Adversary had sent the Aberration to subvert the Master's work. Now, the Adversary could taste the bitter cup of defeat.

The Aberration hung naked with his outstretched hands nailed to the cross and a nail in each of his feet. Two thieves hung upon crosses on either side of him. Clouds rolled in over Jerusalem. Jehuda and several of the Pharisees and scribes stood in a cluster as close as the Roman soldiers would allow them to stand. John and the Aberration's mother were allowed to stand with two other women at the foot of the cross. The Master stood with his arms crossed at the edge of the crowd. The bloodthirsty spectators needed to see the Aberration die. Slowly. Relief and satisfaction radiated from the Master's cold face. He had to see it for himself, too.

His victory.

He had extinguished the last remnant of conscience in Pontius Pilate. He had turned the religious leaders of Jerusalem into murderers. The disciples he turned into cowards. And the Aberration into a corpse. Soon. Already, he had visions of the Aberration suspended in the blackness of the Keep.

The Pharisees cast abuse at the Aberration as he hung bleeding and breathing shallowly. They said they would believe in him if he came down from the cross. The Master laughed heartily. No, they wouldn't. Nothing like kicking a man when he's down. Or nailed to a cross, for that matter. A darkness deeper than the clouds slowly enshrouded the land. The Adversary must be displeased, thought the Master, looking up at the oppressive sky. Let him weep.

His silver eyes turned to the Aberration's mother crying, covering her mouth with a delicate, wrinkled hand. John wept, placing his hands on the poor mother's shoulders.

"Woman," the Aberration said gently, "behold your son." She turned to John, her face wracked with pain. "John," he continued, "behold your mother." John tightened his grip on the weeping woman's shoulders.

The Master's eyes emanated pure bliss. Nothing destroyed a woman so completely as witnessing the death of her child. Exquisite. He would very much like to pay her a visit after this.

149

The Elder stood beside the Master as he watched his defeated foe languish in agony.

"Well done, my Lord. Very well done indeed," the Elder lauded. The Master held his gaze.

"He was almost a worthy opponent," he said triumphantly.

"Almost," repeated the Elder. Gratified silence hung between them for several moments. The sweetness of their triumph was intoxicating. Distant thunder rumbled from the slate colored clouds threatening to sink lower and smother all of Jerusalem. The Elder hazarded a question. "After this, it is back to business as usual?"

"Of course," replied the Master. "Although, it does grant us considerable leverage in our struggle with the Adversary. After all, I have just thwarted his most devious attack on us in the long eons we have been here."

"True," the Elder agreed. His eyes cut over to the Master for a second and then back to the suffering animal nailed to the cross. "We will resume our rightful place, my Lord. And the Adversary will be cast down to his."

The Master nodded and smiled.

"Truer words were never spoken."

With rising excitement, the two voyeurs continued to stare at the bleeding, naked creature asphyxiating slowly. The thief crucified at his left hand glowered at him, venom seeping from his yellowed eyes.

"If you are the Messiah, save yourself and us," he hissed.

The Aberration said nothing.

"Don't you fear God, since you see that we are condemned like him?!" shouted the thief at the Aberration's right hand. "We deserve this for what we've done." He began to cry like a small child. Tears poured down his dirty face. "But this man has done nothing wrong." He looked at the Aberration through his unceasing tears. "Jesus, Lord, remember me when you come into your kingdom."

Painfully, the Aberration looked at him with kindness.

"Truly, I say to you that today you will be with me in paradise."

The Master snickered.

"I don't think you'll call it that when you get there," he said, playfully.

Gasping as the weight of his body pressed down on his pierced feet, the Aberration asked for a drink. One of the soldiers at his feet soaked a sponge with vinegar and stuck it on a hyssop branch, raising it to his parched lips. He sipped at it and leaned his head back against the cross. His battered body could not take much more. To take a breath, he had to push himself up with his feet, and this was becoming increasingly difficult. As we would sink back down, his hands sent a paroxysm of pain through his whole body. His lips were turning blue.

This was it.

Death was near. In a moment, the Aberration would belong to the Master for all eternity. His silver eyes brimmed with tingling anticipation. He took a few steps forward. The heavy air was charged. Mustering a final push upward, the Aberration took a breath and opened his mouth.

"It is finished!" he shouted, his voice carrying loudly over the assembly. His face shone with victory. The Master's excitement changed to confusion. With his head held up regally, the Aberration looked at the Master squarely in the eyes. He stood petrified, sealed hermetically to the ground. Within the Aberration's triumphant stare something else emerged. Something the Master could not discern at first. It grew and grew, until at last, he could identify it. He knew what it was. Pity. The Aberration bowed his head and closed his eyes and breathed his last.

Icy terror paralyzed the Master. The Aberration was dead. He should rejoice. He should sing. But he could not move. A dull grinding roar swelled up from the ground. The earth began to shake with increasing intensity. The Pharisees and scribes fled with the rest of the crowd. Cracking and snapping, the din of rocks bursting filled the people's ears with pain and hearts with fear.

The Guardian appeared before the Master, his golden eyes wide with panic. He boldly took the Master by the wrists.

"My Lord, something is wrong. Come now," he begged in a harried voice.

The Master's terror sharpened. He hesitated
before leaping to the Keep. His eyes shot back to the
Aberration hanging dead on the cross against the
black sky.

+

The Master and the Guardian landed on the
south wall of the Keep. It shook violently. The
earthquake back on earth was strangely magnified in
this space beyond space, this hidden pocket of the
universe. Mass panic ignited among the prisoners.
They stumbled into one another, staring in all
directions with frightened blind eyes. Despite the
darkness, they continued to search frantically for
something, anything that could explain what was
happening. Some cried. Some cursed. Some prayed.
All were shaken.

"Did we lose anyone?" the Master shouted
against the deafening chaos.

The Guardian covered his ears.

"No!" He tried to follow the prisoners' erratic
movements, but could not. They scurried like ants
over a freshly destroyed anthill. "What is
happening?!" he screamed.

No answer.

Cracks burst from the walls which had stood
impregnable for ages, spewing enormous clouds of
dust.

"My Lord!" he shouted.

The ground shuddered with unearthly
intensity. Multiplying cracks tore through the

mighty walls, spidering out in countless directions. The Guardian lost his footing. The section of wall beneath his feet gave way, crashing to the ground with him beside it. Growling furiously, the Master launched himself into the ether above the prisoners' heads at the speed of sound. His ears tuned precisely to the voices he passed while his eyes feverishly scanned faces. Sight and sound registered and were discarded in a wash over him in his search surpassing the limits of desperation.

Qin. Woman. "No!" Baby. Aztec. "Deliver us, Ahura-Mazda." Boy. Babylonian. Olmec. Girl. Man. "We're already dead! What are you talking about?" Hmong. Baby. Igbo. Boy. "Hare Rama! Hare Krishna!" Woman. Man. "God damn!" Celt. Boy. Ming. Baby. Dravidian. Man. Baby. "Oh, please! Please! Mercy!" Woman. Hittite. "Lord have mercy!" Carthaginian. Samaritan. Girl. "Mighty Thor, take pity on us!" Man. Boy. "This is the end!" Woman. Man. Baby. Jew. Sumerian. Boy. "A curse upon you, Pluto!" Comanche. Etruscan. Woman. "Oh, Heart-of-Sky-Heart-of-Earth! Save us!" Boy. Arab. Mongol. Man. Akkadian. "We are lost! We are lost!" Woman. Lombard. Man. Amalekite. Jew.

Found him.

John the Baptist prayed, eyes looking up, arms raised.

"...he leads me in the paths of righteousness for his name's sake..."

154

The Master seized him, pulling his face close to his. Vast segments of wall crumbled to the ground. Debris. Dust. Noise. He screeched in the Baptist' face, his eyes wild with fury.

"What is he doing? Answer me, God damn you!"

"...*Yea, though I walk through the valley of the shadow of death, I will fear no evil, for you are with me...*"

Roaring savagely, the Master cast him several yards away. He leaped on top of him and yanked him back up from the ground with both hands.

"What have *you* done?!"

The Baptist's fiery eyes met his.

"I have prepared the way."

He cast him to the ground. The abyss above began to swirl, sending gusts of powerful winds through the growing gaps in the walls onto the prisoners. Mouth open with shock, the Master forgot the Baptist and was immediately transfixed on the storm above. Never before had the abyss moved. He had always believed it was simply a void, a sea of oblivion. But now he could see that it had substance. That it was *something*. Its endless spiral spun hypnotically. Dust and wind buffeted the Master as he stood, immoveable. From the center of the black maelstrom emerged a speck of gray. A growing orb swelling and spreading. It was undeniable.

Light.

Hideous to behold.

"Fuck!"

Gray spread its slender fingers to the horizons as white light grew from the center, brighter and brighter. For the first time, the prisoners in the Keep could see. Each captive reacted to the gift of sight in his own way. Joy. Hope. Fear. The light hurt the Master's eyes. He fell to his knees squinting, raising his hand to shade his eyes. No longer an abyss, the swirling space above had become a sky, blanketed with cloud, growing brighter. A dazzling pillar of cloud descended slowly.

Brighter.

In a blinding and deafening explosion, the Aberration blasted forth from the pillar, his clothes resplendent, white beyond white, billowing on the wind. His eyes like fire. His face transfigured in unutterable glory, magnificent and terrible. The light did not merely surround him. He *was* the light. Illuminating the farthest reaches of the Keep with the effulgence of countless suns, from horizon to horizon. His feet touched the ground with staggering force, splitting it in four directions as far as the eye could see.

Brighter. Hotter.

Beseechingly, droves of prisoners raised their hands to him, while others crouched, trying to shield their eyes from the burning brightness. In his light, innumerable captives beheld the fulfillment of their being, the answer to their unanswerable questions. Others found in his light the source of all torments, a gnawing monstrosity that would not leave them alone. He pierced the depths of each man, woman, and child held captive. He was warmth and comfort, the satisfaction of deepest yearning. And he was blinding outer darkness, weeping and gnashing of teeth.

The Master's heart split, dissolving in cowardice. Where was his former strength, the insurmountable might by which he had enslaved the entire human race? *What* was it? Here, beneath the crushing weight of this smothering light, it was nothing.

The Aberration landed near an elderly black couple.

"No," the Master said, tremulously.

It was them. The first. The oldest prisoners.

They reached up to the Aberration, their hands shaking, their eyes aglow with the joy they once had long, long ago. He grabbed their wrists and pulled them up, refusing to release them and spoke to all witnessing this spectacle.

"Come to me, all you who labor and are burdened, and I will give you rest."

His towering voice carried loudly into every ear, bringing peace and horror. It suddenly dawned upon the Master why he had always found his voice galling. He had heard it before. Long before the Aberration was born. He remembered.

Those closest to the old couple who themselves also yearned for the light, drew near and placed their hands on them. More approached, placing their hands on another whose hands touched another, all the way to the old couple. John the Baptist joined in, beaming. The little girl from Judea, her ethereal almond eyes radiant with joy, joined in with her mother and father. A complete circuit. The Aberration's light transfigured them as they gathered in communion with one another. Inseparable. The others covered their heads, balled up and isolated in terror. They shut their stinging eyes tightly to no avail. It was inescapable.

Brighter.

Euphoria. Agony.

"NO!" screamed the Master with the last of his strength.

The light burst to its absolute pinnacle, drowning out sound. The Master's form set ablaze, consumed in raging white flames. His screams of bitterest anguish could not be heard through the flood of light. He saw nothing but darkness. He writhed, languishing in fire. Like long ago. Only now, there was nowhere further to fall.

In a flash, the light diminished, the fire extinguished. Still stinging, but no longer burning. Destroyed by pain, the Master opened his eyes. Slowly. The sky still shone, but not too sharply. A light gray. They were gone. All those who reached out to the Aberration were nowhere to be found. Only those who detested the light remained. Still balled up, covering their heads with shaking hands. The Master's mouth and eyes hung open with exhaustion and defeat. With unbearable weariness, he surveyed the landscape. Piles of rubble and loose debris littered the ground as far as the eye could see.

Nothing remained standing of the once behemoth walls. Only sky. Dust blew over the Master and the remaining captives. If they were still captives at all. If they were, then they belonged to him no more. His kingdom was annihilated. Might and glory departed as far as he could see. Desolation.

The wind was the only sound. For hours. He remained kneeling rigidly. His eyes glazed over, staring catatonically ahead. For all of his genius and all of his fortitude, he was utterly at a loss. He had failed catastrophically. He had been certain, so completely certain that his labyrinthine scheming, his hiding in shadows and whispers, his masterful web, was a trap for the Aberration. A trap to show the Adversary that he, the Master, was his equal, if not greater than him. But everything was clear now. No more mysteries. The Master had not set a trap for the Aberration; the Aberration had set a trap for him. The Aberration was not an agent of the Adversary; he *was* the Adversary. And he had won.

Silently, the Elder approached the Master from behind, quaking with fresh fear. The Master rocked slightly on his knees. Eyes hollow. Numb. The Elder began to weep quietly. He stopped three steps behind the Master.

"My Lord."

Wind. Dust.

"My Lord…what are we going to do now?"

Awareness lit the Master's face. His miserable defeat.

A horrific scream ripped the silence asunder. Echoing endlessly.

+

Silent and unresponsive. He did not speak for weeks. The Elder and the rest of the Council stopped trying to ask him questions. He never answered. His cold silver eyes neither blinked nor gave any sign that he heard anything. They figured that when he had something to say, he would say it. Whenever that would be. Moloch directed the Council to resume their duties, as the Elder accompanied the Master on his silent wanderings. Not knowing how to do anything other than watch, the Guardian followed the Elder. Both the Elder and the Guardian hated following him. They did not understand why he kept returning to the same places. It could only bring him pain. Not that they felt any kind of sympathy for him. They simply wanted to minimize the severity of a potential future outburst.

One sunny morning, the Master broke with habit and walked to a mountain in Galilee. The Elder and the Guardian seemed pleased that he was going somewhere different that day. Perhaps he could clear his mind of the troubles which ceaselessly plagued him of late. Once again, they followed him dutifully. There seemed to be a trace of hope in the cloudless sky on this pleasantly warm day. Trekking up the side of the mountain on a rocky trail, the scent of the cedars eluded them, as always, but they found some pleasure in speckled shadows hanging over the path. Their hearts light, they followed him up to a flat, grassy expanse near the top. A cool breeze carried the fragrance of sage from nearby bushes. Red-breasted thrushes and tan warblers sang in the tall cedars and sycamores. The Elder and the Guardian continued into the grass but stopped when they saw where the Master was walking. Their hearts sank.

The distant sound of conversation and laughter filled them with frustrated disappointment. The Master had gone to see them again. Fifty yards away, the disciples sat talking in a circle. Among them were the Aberration's mother and several other followers from his outer circle. And he was with them, too. The Aberration. He was listening intently to a story told by Thomas. He smiled and nodded. The Elder and the Guardian sighed and turned and walked heavily away. They could not bear to watch any more of this. The Master, however, stayed. Watching and listening sourly.

Answering a question, the Aberration reached over to Peter and squeezed his shoulder. There was no resentment here, no sorrow or foul memory. Only friendship and warmth. The Master had forgotten completely that Judas Iscariot was no longer part of the circle. It did not matter. What did matter and what now made life unbearable should still be dead and festering in his grave. But he was here. Alive. Indestructible. He told the disciples that they needed to wait in Jerusalem for the Holy Spirit, who would come to them from the Father. This Holy Spirit, whoever he was, would give them power, and they would bear witness of the Aberration to the entire world. People would hear about him. They would see that his followers could perform the same works he performed. And they would see that his followers loved one another, those close to them, and their enemies the same way he loved them.

It was too much to bear.

The Aberration stood slowly and looked intently, lovingly at his disciples and his mother — his friends. Silence hung between them, imbued with joy and love. Wordlessly, they bowed before him in worship. Now, they knew who he was. So did the Master. He still stung. The Aberration spoke, his voice rankling the core of the Master's being.

"All power is given to me in heaven and in earth. Therefore, go and teach all nations, baptizing them in the name of the Father, and of the Son, and of the Holy Spirit, teaching them to observe all things which I have commanded you."

Their hearts burned within them. Tears welled in the eyes of some. He looked on them with tenderness, seeing their devotion. And he would not leave them without comfort.

"I am with you always, even unto the end of the world. Amen."

His feet left the ground as he ascended upward into the heavens. The disciples and the Master followed him with their eyes as far as he remained in sight. They stood. Even after he was no longer visible, they continued to stare into the sky above, searching for some trace of him in the clear blue. The Master felt only crushing emptiness. He is gone, he thought, only he's not. A voice startled him.

"Men of Galilee..."

The Master snapped to the source of the voice. What an odd surprise. It was Michael from long ago. And Gabriel stood beside him.

"...why do you stand, gazing up into heaven? This same Jesus will come back to you in the manner that you saw him go up."

"It figures," mumbled the Master.

He surprised himself. These were the first words he had spoken in weeks. He turned his back on the disciples and his former partners and walked down the mountain. With each step, his thoughts became clearer. Fear and devastation remained, but at least he could think through them now. He began to understand the magnitude of the Adversary's campaign against him. To ensure that he had everything perfectly straight, he spoke his thoughts aloud. To the Adversary.

"I thought you had abandoned the project you started with the talking apes. What was it that that Moses of yours wrote in his book? *'Let us make man in our image, after our likeness'*? How fucking poetic. You were after that all along, weren't you? You gave them the image. The reason, the free will. But they had to grow into the likeness themselves. I knew I couldn't destroy the image, but the likeness, I knew I could stop that from happening. And I did. For ages and ages. I ruined your plans for them. You wanted

163

them to choose immortality, but I got them to choose
death. Like animals. They *are* fucking animals! But
then you finished it. All the disease, all the poison
they inflict on themselves, now it can be undone.
And now they can become like you. Like you always
wanted. You arrogant bastard!"

For the remainder of the day, he walked and
leaped alone, avoiding populated areas. No one
from the Council tried to seek him out. He crossed
deserts and forests, immersed in thought. As the sun
began to sink in the west, he found himself in a
meadow. The tall deep green grass and wildflowers
undulated in the wind. A single monarch butterfly,
its brilliant orange and black wings beating on the
wind, fluttered toward him. His pale hand snatched
it from the air as quickly as a snake bite. He cradled
it and slowly began to close his arching fingers over
it. He stopped. Looking up, away from the butterfly,
he thought for a moment. His gaze returned to the
insect in his hand.
He opened his fingers and let it flutter away, smiling
malignantly.

+

Hills and ridges of ice enclosed and
occasionally punctuated miles of flat, frozen terrain.
Vacant. The dry air lay dead, suspended in the half-
light under the plutonian gray sky. No living thing
would dare approach the edge of this treacherous
waste, which spanned thousands of miles. The
Council waited silently for the Master to arrive.

Untouched by the cold, they stood frozen with foreboding. There was no way this meeting could go well. Tension accumulated like frost with the passage of time. This must be what it felt like to wait with bent neck under the executioner's sword, thought the Elder.

The Master arrived in their midst.

"Hail, Lord!" they shouted, unable to hide their trepidation.

He took slow, measured steps over the ice, holding his head erect with an air of unshakable resolve. No one moved. Every member of the Council was certain that even the blink of an eye would stir the air into a hurricane which would consume them all. His ominous form looming over soundless footfalls gave the impression of a beast, sleek and muscular, passing by prey trying desperately to hold still. At last, his voice sliced through the silence, colder than the uninhabitable hell in which they stood.

"The nature of the war has changed," he paused, "completely."

Petrified silence.

"Sadly, death is no longer the end for the vermin we have hunted for so long. The Adversary has made a way out of it. If the Aberration's resurrection has shown us anything, it is that he will one day reconstitute each and every one of these creatures. And not simply as they were when they perished, but in a new and indestructible form."

The Council's terror remained like a breath held beyond the limits of endurance, stretching and swelling to escape.

"When he began to create them, I was certain that I had arrested the process, stopped it altogether, leaving them a race of hobbled, unfinished clay dolls. And since that time, it has been our great pleasure to smash them to pieces." He paused again. "Personally, I always preferred to pull them apart piece by piece." The side of his mouth twitched. "But the Aberration, or should I say, the *Adversary* has finished what he began to create—a real human." He laughed slightly, closing his eyes and shaking his head.

The piercing anxiety did not subside. It was simply sharpened by disbelief.

"Our goal has changed. Death is impermanent and, therefore, irrelevant. What is relevant now is the *creation*."

Asmodeus could not keep quiet. He needed to understand.

"The creation, my Lord?"

The Master faced him, stretching taller with reptilian grace.

"The creation. The Adversary finished the creation of humankind in the Aberration. Now, he extends the completion of creation to every human being. They can all become what he meant them to become."

Gasps of disbelief and despair issued from each Council member. The weight of their defeat fell in full force upon them.

"My Lord," began the Elder, despairingly, "what is there left to do? He has taken everything. Everything! Why should we not go before him now and beg for annihilation? What can we do in the face of such desolation?! We have los..."

The Master thrust him to the ground, placing his foot on the Elder's chest as he lay flat on his back.

"Because, you loathsome bootlicker, there is a better way!"

He stepped over the Elder who did not dare to get up. His silver eyes teemed with pure inspiration.

"He has already saved them from death. He offers to save them from their failures and weaknesses as well. But therein lies the problem and our advantage. They have to want it."

He bent slightly and extended his pale hand to the Elder, who took it hesitantly. He pulled him to his feet.

"They have to believe, first. You saw it yourselves that there were thousands who saw the things he did and did not believe in him. Even after he appeared to them, having risen from the dead! And there will continue to be people who see miraculous wonders performed by his followers, but who will not believe. This is where we come in. Convince those who witness such works that it is merely chance or that some other force is at work."

He turned and paced within the circle, passing by each member.

"His followers will spread the news of his sojourn here on earth, his death, his resurrection, his impending return, and the news will spread like a plague. We must inspire both them and those not affiliated with them to make the Aberration in their own image, after *their* likeness. Turn him into a teacher, a prophet, a philosopher, a good man, a villain. Take away his humanity. Or his divinity. Confuse the two or separate them. It really doesn't matter. So long as they don't recognize him as the Adversary become flesh.

"And even if they believe that, we can still improve upon the idea. Change the Adversary's motivation. Tell them he became human to satisfy an angry and spiteful Father whose thirst for revenge could never be slaked even if he drank the blood of the entire human race. Or tell them he came to satisfy justice, which is somehow *greater* than the Adversary. Change the cross from an act of mercy into an act of justice. Make sin the Adversary's problem, not humanity's problem."

The Council followed every word, drawn gradually into the depths of his curiously brilliant plan.

"Get between his followers. He said that everyone would know that they were his disciples by their love for one another. Tear them apart with enmity. Take their focus off of the Aberration, and get them to behave no differently than those who have never heard of him. Hold up their failures and crimes for the world to see as evidence that the Aberration's time on earth is nothing more than a folk tale made up by savages, another story for children.

"For those on the outside who hear the message, draw their attention to the horrors of life. Focus them on the cruelty of their fellow creatures and on the cold, unresponsive nature of the universe. Have them believe that there is nothing worse than an empty belly and nothing as unjust as an early grave. Let them ask how a loving, all-powerful deity could possibly allow such evils in the world, but do *not* let them ask how they are able to determine what is good and what is evil. Prevent them from asking such prickly questions."

The Master pointed a commanding finger at the dim sky.

"The sun will soon come up after hiding for half the year, and the aurora will do its customary dance of glowing color. But when it does, you will not be able to see it clearly because of the cloud cover. And so it is with the Aberration's work. It will shine brightly, but we will obscure it. The Adversary has just completed his last great work. And now, I am starting mine."

No trace of fear remained in the pale faces of the Council. Zeal and determination had driven it out. One by one, they fell down and worshipped the Master. Chin raised, chest out, eyes looking down on his sycophants as they paid him his due, the Master lifted himself into the air. Their devotion fueled the inextinguishable flame of his pride, burning recklessly in his heart and in his eyes. His unconquerable will covered them as a shadow, an abysmal call to prayer.

"There is no God but me, and you are my prophets. There is no truth that I cannot make a lie. No love that I cannot twist into hatred. No light that I cannot bury in darkness. My new kingdom will be born both in hearts fiery with hatred and cold with indifference. You are my witnesses. Go. And prepare my way."

They vanished one after another. Only the Master remained, still aloft on the frozen air. He felt the urge to take out the little leather bag again. Holding it tightly, he waited, expecting another wave of inspiration or some new revelation about the road ahead of him. He waited. But it never came. Disappointment filled him as he looked at the little pouch, coming down to the ground. Once a trophy proclaiming his glory, it was now only a memento of defeat. Worthless. He cast it as far from him as he could and started to walk in the opposite direction, but stopped.

"I will never be rid of you, and you will never be rid of me. But you will learn your place," he said. The wind began to howl, and he leaped out of the frozen waste. So much work to do and so little time.